IDITAROD NIGHTS

IDITAROD NIGHTS

Cindy Hiday

Ooligan Press

Portland, Oregon

Iditarod Nights
© 2020 Cindy Hiday

ISBN13: 978-1-947845-13-8

Ooligan Press
Portland State University
Post Office Box 751, Portland, Oregon 97207
503.725.9748
ooligan@ooliganpress.pdx.edu
www.ooliganpress.pdx.edu

Library of Congress Cataloging-in-Publication Data
Names: Hiday, Cindy, 1954- author.
Title: Iditarod nights / Cindy Hiday.
Description: Portland, Oregon : Ooligan Press, [2020] | Series: Ooligan Press Library Writers Project collection
Identifiers: LCCN 2019039336 | ISBN 9781947845138 (paperback) | ISBN 9781947845145 (ebook)
Subjects: LCSH: Iditarod (Race)--Fiction. | Sled dog racing--Alaska--Fiction. | Nome (Alaska)--Fiction.
Classification: LCC PS3608.I296 I35 2020 | DDC 813/.6--dc23 LC record available at https://lccn.loc.gov/2019039336

Cover design by Des Hewson
Interior design by Kendra Ferguson

References to website URLs were accurate at the time of writing. Neither the author nor Ooligan Press is responsible for URLs that have changed or expired since the manuscript was prepared.

Printed in the United States of America

Library Writers Project

Ooligan Press and Multnomah County Library have created a unique partnership celebrating the Portland area's local authors. Each fall since 2015, Multnomah County Library has solicited submissions of self-published works of fiction by local authors to be added to its Library Writers Project ebook collection. Multnomah County Library and Ooligan Press have partnered to bring these previously ebook-only works to print. *Iditarod Nights* is the second in an annual series of Library Writers Project books to be published by Ooligan Press. To learn more about the Library Writers Project, visit https://multcolib.org/library-writers-project.

Ooligan Press Library Writers Project Collection

Iditarod Nights by Cindy Hiday (2020)
The Gifts We Keep by Katie Grindeland (2019)

Dedicated to the men and women of the Iditarod.
And the dogs.
Always the dogs.

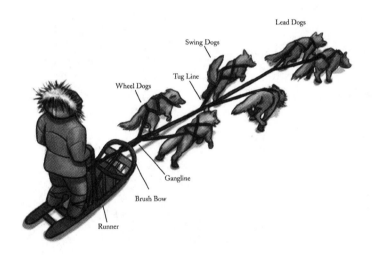

Lead Dogs

Swing Dogs

Tug Line

Wheel Dogs

Gangline

Brush Bow

Runner

Dog Sled and Team

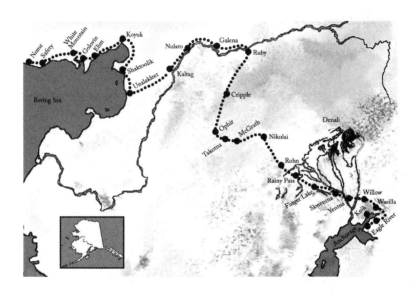

Iditarod Trail (Northern Route)

Preface

Each year on the first Saturday of March, a diverse group of passionate men and women from around the world converge with their teams of four-legged athletes in Anchorage, Alaska, for the start of the Iditarod Trail Sled Dog Race. From there, they attempt to make their way across a thousand miles of the state's most striking, challenging terrain, battling harsh weather conditions and sleep deprivation to reach the burled arch in Nome, Alaska, on the coast of the Bering Sea. Some compete to be first; for many, the goal is simply to finish, to go the distance, no matter how long it takes—without losing a dog. The training is intense, the exhaustion extreme, the rewards life altering.

Chapter 1

"What do you mean he's not coming?" Claire asked. The bitter smell of stale coffee assaulted her sinuses as she unzipped her parka in the heat of the cramped air taxi office. It was bad enough she'd been coerced by her matchmaker friend into driving to Talkeetna to pick up some man she'd never met; she didn't need complications. "I saw animal carriers being unloaded when I pulled in."

"Weren't his," George, the whip-thin sixty-year-old flight service owner, replied. His office chair gave a rusty squawk as he leaned across his desk and handed Claire a slip of yellow notepaper. "Got the call about ten minutes ago. Some of his dogs came down with kennel cough."

"Oh." Claire's irritation gave way to concern. The canine malady was a highly contagious respiratory infection that could develop into pneumonia if not properly treated. She glanced at the note. *Antibiotics and rest. Tell Matt and Janey I'll see them next year.*

"He apologized for not getting word to you sooner," George said. "Guess he was hoping the dogs would pull out of it in time to make the trip."

"He must be terribly disappointed." Claire had put her career on hold for two years to train and qualify for the Iditarod; to have to withdraw ten days before the race would be heartbreaking. But the Alaskan bush was no place for a sick dog. She shoved the note into the pocket of her parka. "Well then, I suppose that's—"

The office door blew open, cutting her off. A surge of frigid Alaskan air entered on the heels of a tall figure in a forest-green parka and moose-hide mukluks laced up to the knees of his faded jeans. His dark-brown hair swept back from his face untamed. As he moved away from the door, his eyes, as clear blue as glacier ice, surveyed the small room, cataloging his surroundings: a learned habit Claire had seen before. Law enforcement would be her guess. His gaze settled on her, and an unexpected rush of heat prickled the skin beneath her thick flannel shirt.

George asked, "Can I help you?"

Those intense eyes held Claire's a second longer, then shifted to George. "I'm looking for Ted Warren," he said, a raw huskiness in his voice.

"You just get off the plane from Nome?" George asked.

"That's right."

The older man referred to another slip of paper. "You must be Dillon Cord."

"Yes."

George shoved his knit cap higher on his forehead, exposing a thick shock of white hair. "I'm afraid Ted won't be showing. He's in intensive care at Providence Hospital down in Anchorage."

Claire drew a sharp breath. Ted and Sarah Warren were her neighbors. "What happened?"

"Heart attack, late last night," George replied. "His wife called just a bit ago from the hospital."

"What's his condition?"

"He's stabilized—that's all Sarah could tell me." George returned his attention to Dillon Cord. "You a friend of Ted's?"

"No. Somebody I know put me in touch with him. I had arrangements to board my team at his place until the race."

"Those were your dogs I saw being unloaded," Claire said.

"Yes, ma'am." Fatigue pulled at the lines around his mouth. "Would either of you know where I can put up sixteen dogs?"

Claire didn't waste time analyzing the feeling that some force beyond her control had taken charge of the moment. "I was supposed to pick up a musher and his team from Teller," she said, "but I just got word he won't be coming. The vacancy is yours if you want it."

She could have called Janey and Matt first, but she knew her friends well enough to have a good idea what they'd say. It helped that Ted and Sarah had been willing to take the other man in, but Claire relied on her intuition more than anything else. After seven years in criminal defense, she considered herself an accurate judge of character.

Except when it comes to my personal life, she thought bitterly.

George leaned back, causing his chair to shriek again. "Well, Mr. Cord, looks like this is your lucky day. Matt and Janey Sommer run a top-notch operation, and they're only a couple miles down the road. Claire here's been training at their kennel. She'll be a rookie in this year's race."

"Are you sure I won't be imposing?"

Claire gave a wry smile. The musher she'd been sent to meet, according to Janey, was thirty-seven, good looking, and single. Dillon Cord appeared to be in the same age group, maybe a couple years younger, and, in her opinion, he met the second criterion. She wasn't going to ask about the third. "My friends are expecting me to bring back a musher and his dogs," she told him. "You'll be asked to help with chores and contribute a little for groceries, but the bunk in the cookhouse is free. Of course, you're responsible for your own dogs' chow."

"In that case, I accept," he said, and smiled.

Claire's breath caught. *Maybe this isn't such a good idea,* she thought. But the sensation didn't last. She was more than capable of guarding her heart against a man's attractive smile—she'd had two years of practice. A strand of hair had worked itself free from the braid at the back of her head, and she tucked it behind her ear. "As George said, I think you'll be happy with the arrangement."

"I'll help you load your dogs." George made to stand just as his telephone rang. "Darn thing. Hang on a minute."

"That's all right," Claire said. "You take care of business. I'm sure the two of us can manage."

The older man gave Dillon a quick sizing up, then nodded. "S'pose you're right. Give my best to Matt and Janey." He shot Claire a wink and reached for the phone.

"I'll do that." She turned toward the door. Dillon reached it first and held it open for her. "Thank you," she said, embarrassed by how feminine his simple gesture made her feel; men had opened doors for her before.

Just not lately.

Stepping out of the overheated office, she zipped her jacket and pulled on her insulated gloves. The cold, dry air purged the smell of old coffee from her nose. A thermometer mounted to the outside of the building read fifteen degrees; the low afternoon sun shone bright against a new layer of powdery snow dusting the airstrip. Dillon's dogs, still in their airline carriers in front of the hangar, yipped and barked when they saw him.

"It's all right, kids," he called. "Not much longer now." The racket quieted to intermittent whines.

The Sommers' truck was an old one-ton Ford pickup, its bed an enclosed wooden box divided into twenty compartments—two levels of five on each side—with space down the middle for equipment.

"Have you run the Iditarod before?" Claire asked as she helped him stow harnesses, lines, and personal gear between the compartments. The sleds—a toboggan and a lighter sprinter—went on top of the dog box.

"Twice."

"Mind if I ask how you did?"

"I made it to Nome both times."

Claire gave a light laugh. "I can only hope for as much." She found a space for his snowshoes and secured the rear compartment. "Let's get those kids of yours loaded."

He led a blue-eyed white Siberian husky from the first airline carrier and hefted her into one of the truck's top compartments, murmuring unintelligible endearments to the dog while he worked.

You can tell a lot about a man by how he treats his dogs, Claire thought, and felt that unexpected rush of heat again. She shifted and cleared her throat. "Beautiful dog."

"Bonnie's my best leader. Not the fastest, but I can depend on her." He nodded toward a carrier containing another Siberian, this one with a tan blaze on its muzzle. "That character over there is her brother Clyde."

"Bonnie and Clyde?"

"When they were pups, they'd steal anything they could get in their mouths." He shot her a half smile that made her pulse miss a beat.

"Thanks for the warning. If something comes up missing, I'll know where to look."

But judging by her reaction to the man—and what she suspected Janey would say when she got a look at him—Claire had a feeling Bonnie and Clyde might be the least of her worries.

Riding in the passenger seat of the Ford, Dillon gazed out the window at the frozen banks of the Susitna River and the snow-covered Alaska Range in the distance. Talkeetna was located at the end of a fourteen-mile paved spur branching off Parks Highway, the main route to Denali National Park. A brief break in the clouds shrouding the highest mountain in North America— Denali—gave him a glimpse of its sharp, arresting peaks before it slipped under cover again.

But the trees interested him more: cottonwood, birch, spruce, and alder, their branches struggling to support thick layers of snow. This was another world compared to the flat black sand beaches of Nome. He had his work cut out for him getting his team accustomed to running in dense vegetation. He should have started sooner, but money and time were tight.

He glanced over at the woman sitting beside him, her gloved hands wrapped firmly around the steering wheel as she squinted against the glare of the lowering sun. The truck was heavy with sixteen huskies and all his gear in the back, but Dillon had a feeling she could handle it. This may have been her first Iditarod, but she had a certain self-assurance about her, a determined set to her chin. Though she was slender, her features suggested the kind of athletic strength that came from hours of training a team of dogs. She wore her light-blond hair in a braid that disappeared beneath the collar of her parka. When she pulled off a glove to push a strand of it behind her ear, he saw her work-roughened hand. Then, apparently deciding the cab had warmed up enough, she removed her other glove and dropped them both on the bench seat. Her gaze caught his for an instant before returning to the road.

Her dark-amber eyes reminded him of aged whiskey.

"What do you do in Nome, Dillon?"

A heartbeat passed while he put a damper on his reaction to those eyes. "I own a bar and grill: the Bering West."

She shot him a quick look of surprise. "Oh, I thought maybe you…"

Dillon waited, already suspecting what she was going to say. He knew he retained habits from his former life that some people picked up on more readily than others. Things like hypervigilance had been trained into him and would be a part of him for as long as he lived.

"I'm sorry," she said with a self-conscious flick of her hand on the steering wheel. "It's not important." She worried her lower lip between her teeth as if calculating her next question. Finally, she gave a sigh that bordered on exasperation and asked, "Are you married?"

"No."

The abruptness of his answer earned him another quick look. "I didn't mean to be nosy." She muttered something Dillon couldn't make out, then went on to explain, "It's just that there's something you should know about my friend."

The strand of hair she'd tucked behind her ear came loose again, and she brushed it away from her face. A nervous habit, Dillon realized.

"Janey and I have known each other since grade school. When she married Matt and moved to Alaska, we didn't see each other for years." She shot him a resigned smile. "Now that I'm here, she doesn't want me to leave."

The truck sideslipped around a slick, shadowy curve. Dillon tensed, his thoughts flying to his dogs riding in the back. But before he could make a sound, Claire eased back on the throttle and corrected the slide with a slight turn of the wheel.

She continued without missing a beat. "Janey is set on finding me a husband while I'm here so I'll stay in Alaska after the race." Her voice reflected her irony. "I'm afraid she's going to take one look at you and have me off to Anchorage to try on wedding dresses."

Her statement was so outrageous and unexpected, Dillon couldn't contain his abrupt laugh. "Should I consider that a compliment?"

He caught her gaze again. Before she tucked her eyes away beneath lowered lashes, he saw a flash of acknowledgment that sent a bolt of something hot and alive through his body. When was the last time a woman had affected him that way?

He released a slow, thoughtful breath.

"Consider it a warning," Claire replied with a dismissive shrug. "Janey's a born matchmaker, and her determination can be indomitable. Why do you think I was sent to pick up the musher from Teller?"

"Because he's single."

"Bingo."

"But you're not interested."

"I didn't come to Alaska to get married," she stated. "I just wish I could convince Janey of that."

Dillon knew it was none of his business, but he couldn't resist asking. "Why *did* you come to Alaska?"

A slew of emotions crossed her features before she settled on one: defiance. "To run the Iditarod," she said, giving him a direct look. "You don't have a problem with women competing, do you?"

Dillon's mind detoured. As his gaze drifted to her lips, he could think of a lot of things that might become a problem between them; her choice to risk her neck in the world's toughest sled dog race wasn't one of them. "No, ma'am."

Her grin was immediate, and he felt another jolt of heat wash through him. "Good. I'd hate to have to stop the truck and make you walk. Janey would never forgive me. And please, call me Claire."

"Are you always this tough, Claire?"

"It has its advantages over soft and vulnerable."

He caught himself looking at her again. He was pretty sure she'd intended the remark to sound offhanded, but he wondered if there wasn't more to it.

After a pause, she added, "Especially if you're an attorney."

A dark memory stirred. "An attorney."

"Criminal defense. I'm on a leave of absence from Stanfield,

Wood, and Keller in Portland, Oregon." She glanced over at him. "Have you ever been to Portland?"

Shit, what are the odds? He hesitated for half a beat. "No."

He didn't consider it much of a lie. He'd buried that Dillon Cord when he boarded a plane to Alaska six years ago. The man he'd been, the one from Portland, no longer existed.

Chapter 2

Claire caught Dillon watching her, his blue eyes cool—analytical. She frowned and looked away. Maybe he'd learned to study people who came into his bar, sizing them up as potential troublemakers, but something told her his brain stored information in the same efficient way Maggie, her legal assistant at the firm, filed court papers. He may run a bar and grill now, but he hadn't always.

Had she made a mistake trusting him? After all, what did she really know about the guy?

"I appreciate what you're doing for me," he said.

The weariness had crept back into his voice. She slanted him another quick look. His features were no less taut, his gaze just as direct, but her apprehension that she might have misjudged him disappeared. He had to be exhausted. Returning her attention to the road, she said, "Actually, we're doing each other a favor."

"How is that?"

"With you around, Janey won't have a reason to send me on any more errands involving eligible men." Of course, Claire couldn't dismiss the fact that the man sitting next to her seemed perfectly eligible and far too good looking. She could only be thankful they both had a common goal. "While you and I are concentrating on the race, my friend can have her little fantasies."

"All completely innocent, of course."

Something in his tone drew her gaze. Her pulse surged. There was nothing innocent in those eyes. "Of course." She forced herself to look away, blinked, and realized she was about to miss their turnoff. Muttering an oath, she pumped the brakes and made a left onto a snow-covered gravel drive. A few moments later, Sommer Kennels came into view.

Claire had come to think of the single-story log cabin as home. It was nestled among the trees, with snowshoes hanging from a wide covered porch and a pair of moose antlers mounted over the rough-cut front door. Half a dozen other buildings of varying sizes and materials, used for storage and to protect equipment from the weather, spread out over five acres. The cookhouse—the only other log structure—stood between the cabin and the puppy pen.

She pulled up next to the dog yard and shut off the engine. "Here we are."

A cacophony of yips and howls and excited barks greeted them as forty-two huskies strained against their stake-out chains. Singer's distinctive melody rose above the others; the happy brown-and-black husky's masked face tipped skyward while his brother Riley looked on, grinning. Handsome stood on the flat roof of his house, his white chest proud against his long black body. His symmetrical brows were lifted above his blue eyes, and his long tail curled in a pleased wave. The Ford swayed on its springs as Dillon's dogs shifted in the back and added their own voices to the growing bedlam.

The cabin door banged open and a boy bounded down the steps toward them, his dark hair flying and a parka hanging partway off his skinny frame. "Auntie Claire's back!" he shouted.

Claire smiled. "That's Janey and Matt's eight-year-old son, Andy. I'm not really his aunt, but since Janey and I are like sisters…" She pointed to the petite, slender woman wearing jeans and an insulated vest zipped up over an eye-popping red sweater. Her short brunette hair fanned out from her ruddy face as she rushed after the boy, waving a comb. "There's Janey."

A broad-chested man in faded yellow coveralls and a dingy purple cap emerged from the cookhouse and shouted, "Pipe down over there!" The noise level in the kennel yard dropped to a smattering of whines and low grumbles.

"And that's her husband, Matt."

The driver's-side door flew open and Andy hopped onto the truck's running board, using the steering wheel as a handhold. "Hi!" he said, loud enough to make Claire wince. "My name's Andy!"

Before Claire could ask the boy to lower his voice, Dillon slid his arm across the back of the seat, brushing her shoulders. A current jagged through her, leaving her tongue-tied.

He extended his other arm in front of her. "Nice to meet you, Andy. My name's Dillon."

Andy thrust his hand into Dillon's much larger one and pumped it twice, a look of self-importance on his young face. "Nice to meet you too."

Dillon drew back and Claire took a long, slow breath, flustered by his nearness.

"Andrew Sommer, get down from there and comb your hair," Janey scolded, coming up behind her son.

Andy sighed but did as his mother said.

Janey glanced inside the cab. Her hazel eyes focused on Dillon and widened, her brows disappearing beneath her feathered bangs. "Oh. You're not Lucas."

Dillon smiled. "No, ma'am." He cocked his head and met Claire's gaze. Claire's throat went dry when she saw the bold glint in his eyes. "I'm not married, either."

Heat rocketed up Claire's neck and into her cheeks. For long seconds she stared at him, flabbergasted. When she finally looked away, her gaze collided with Janey's. She wasn't sure which was worse: Dillon's audacity or the wedding bells she knew were ringing in her friend's ears.

"What's going on?" Matt asked, coming to stand behind his wife. He stroked his beard and looked at Dillon. "Who's Claire's friend?"

"I'm not sure," Janey answered, her pert mouth curving into a mischievous grin. "But I can't wait to find out."

Dillon had been unable to resist teasing Claire just a little, given the comical situation he found himself at the center of. He knew teasing a criminal defense attorney was like playing

Russian roulette with a fully loaded revolver. Annoyance radiated from the woman like static electricity.

But the rush of color to her high, smooth cheeks had been worth it.

Once they were out of the truck and introductions had been made, Matt told him, "We'll board your team in those empty doghouses over there," and pointed to a far corner of the kennel yard.

"If you'll excuse me," Claire said, "I have some things to take care of inside." Without another word, she turned and walked away.

Even with her parka hanging below the curve of her hips, she had a way of moving that drew Dillon's attention, her shoulders pulled back, her long stride confident. She didn't go straight to the cabin, stopping to hug a striking Alaskan husky whose legs turned to rubber at the woman's murmurings. The dog rolled onto his back, exposing his white belly to her, and she gave a light, intimate laugh that hit Dillon in a dozen unexpected places. He looked away and found Janey watching him with a wide smile.

"It's good to have you with us, Dillon," she said, her voice bright. "I think you'll be comfortable here."

He wouldn't call it *comfortable* to be thrown off balance by a lawyer he'd already succeeded in irritating. But he'd get over it. "I'm sure I will, ma'am. Thank you."

"Janey. Please." She exchanged a look with her husband. "I'll go put some coffee on while you get our guest settled."

Matt kissed her soundly on the mouth. "Thanks, honey." He chuckled as his wife made a detour on her way to the cabin, snagging Claire's arm and dragging her inside. "So, Dillon," he said once the women were out of earshot, "you ever considered getting married?"

The arid draft of a memory brushed through him. "Not in a long time."

"Then watch yourself, my friend, unless you've a mind to start thinking about it."

"I'll do that."

Andy stood at the back of the truck, carrying on a conversation with one of the dogs through the compartment door cutout. "That's Rocky," Dillon said, moving to stand beside him.

The boy's face scrunched as he peered up at Dillon and asked, "Because he's a fighter, like that guy in the movies?"

Dillon smiled. "No, because he's got a head like a rock wall."

He introduced the rest of the dogs as they were unloaded: Bonnie and Clyde; Deshka, a small, tireless caramel-colored Alaskan husky; mild-tempered Blackie and his agile brother Chevron; a blue-eyed gray-and-white Siberian named Pete; Guy, a big half-hound who was dependable and steady though not very bright; Dodge; Windy; Elliot, another small dog with amazing stamina; and the wheel dogs, Max and Alpine Annie. Flannigan's Stew, Maverick, and Gretchen rounded out the team.

The Sommers' dogs greeted each new visitor, some growling at the intrusion, some standing on their hind legs and yanking at their stake-out chains to sniff the air and whine. A few curled into tight balls, turning their backs to the commotion as if annoyed or simply disinterested. Every dog had a food dish, a low square shelter lined with straw, and a five-foot chain that allowed it to move around without tangling with the others. All the comforts of home.

Dillon could say the same for his own accommodations. The cookhouse was clean and organized, with a bunk suspended from the wall at each side of the door, a cupboard to stow his gear in, and a wood-burning stove in the middle of the room. The only amenity lacking was a bathroom.

"You share the one in the house with us," Andy informed him.

"We keep a fire going out here to heat water for the dogs," Matt went on to explain. "The chow is stored in the back room."

"Most of mine is sitting over at the Warren place," Dillon said. "I had it flown in a couple days ago."

"You can take the Land Cruiser in the morning and pick it up," Matt replied. "I'd go with you, but I have some folks scheduled for a dogsled ride in Talkeetna tomorrow. I'm a tour guide part time."

"Just point me in the right direction."

Matt nodded. "I'll give their son, Brian, a call to let him know you're coming. In the meantime," he said, giving Dillon a companionable slap on the back, "let's water your dogs and go rescue Claire from my wife."

"So this good-looking man walks in needing a place to stay," Janey said as she poured water into the coffee maker, "and you invite him here without thinking twice about it?"

Claire had her head in the refrigerator as she sorted through the vegetable bin for salad ingredients—precious commodities in February. Janey had spared no expense. "That's what I said."

"And you asked him if he was married?"

The disbelief in her friend's voice was understandable. Claire had a little trouble believing it herself. She pushed the refrigerator door shut with her hip and deposited an armload of produce on the kitchen counter. "I knew if I didn't, you would," she stated in her own defense.

"A knockout like that, you bet I would." Janey flipped on the coffee maker and moved to the oven. "You know what this is, don't you?"

"A pot roast?"

"Fate."

Claire sighed. So much for avoiding the inevitable. "It's nothing more than a coincidence," she said, although it hadn't felt that way when she first laid eyes on Dillon in the air taxi office.

Janey leaned against the counter, arms folded in silent observation. Claire's jaw tightened. She'd just about had all the scrutiny she could stomach in one day. "Please don't make a big deal out of this, Janey. You know how I feel about—"

"Alaskan men. I know. Are you sure it's just *Alaskan* men you're shy of?"

Claire stared at her. "I am not shy."

"Bad choice of words." Janey gave a dismissive flick of her hand. "I meant to say you're *disinclined* to have a relationship with any man, Alaskan or otherwise."

Claire scowled and took a peeler to the carrots. "There's nothing wrong with being cautious."

"Call it what you want," her friend remarked. "And I'm sorry I brought it up." She pushed away from the counter. "I'd better make sure we've got enough towels in the bathroom. Our guest looks like he might need an extra one for those broad shoulders."

Claire could only sigh as Janey waggled her eyebrows at her and headed down the hall.

Dillon detected the aromas of roasting beef, garlic, and potatoes as he followed the Sommer men inside and hung his parka and holster by the door. The front of the cabin was a long, open room with a family area at one end, a kitchen at the other, and a cast-iron stove square in the middle. Bright reds, purples, and blues colored the windows and furnishings.

Claire stood at the kitchen counter chopping carrots, her back to him. Her braided hair brushed her nape and stopped high between her shoulder blades; her blue flannel shirt was tucked into slim jeans. His gaze lingered on the narrowness of her waist, the curve of her hips, the length of her legs. She'd traded her chunky rubber boots for well-worn pink slippers. One of them looked like it might have been used as a dog's chew toy.

"Have a seat," Janey said, yanking Dillon from his thoughts. His hostess emerged from a hallway at the rear of the cabin and breezed toward the kitchen. "We were just about to set out dinner. I hope you brought your appetite."

Dillon's glance swung back to Claire. Unsettled by the direction his thoughts were taking, he quickly looked away. "I'll wash up."

Chapter 3

Claire sat across the dinner table from Dillon and wondered what he was thinking. Except for "coffee would be fine, black please," and a polite remark about the food, he maintained a quiet presence in the midst of a boisterous family settling down to dinner.

"Claire?"

"Hmm?" She glanced at Matt and saw him trying to hand her the salad. "Oh," she said, and took the bowl from him.

"It's a darn shame about Ted," Matt said as he scooped mashed potatoes onto his plate. "You sure he's going to be all right?"

"I called Sarah at the hospital," Janey replied, crossing the room with a platter of sliced roast. She handed it to Dillon and took her seat at the other end of the table. "She said the doctor wants to keep him for another day for observation, but there doesn't seem to be any permanent damage."

"How's Sarah holding up?" Claire asked. She passed the salad to Andy, who promptly passed it on to his mother without taking any.

Janey scooped up a large helping with the tongs and dumped it onto the boy's plate. Andy opened his mouth to protest, then closed it at the don't-argue-with-me look his mother leveled at him. "The poor woman sounded exhausted." Janey put some salad on her own plate and made room on the table for the bowl. "She's been at the hospital since last night. She's worried about Brian and the house."

"Brian's seventeen," Claire said. "He should be able to take care of the place for a few days."

"Just the same, I thought I'd make up a food box and run it over to him tomorrow, check on things."

Andy squeezed the bottle of ranch dressing over his salad. "Does that mean I don't have to have lessons tomorrow?"

Claire suppressed her smile, knowing it would earn her a frown from Janey. The boy was homeschooled, and though he was an intelligent kid with a knack for retaining information, he still jumped at any opportunity to get out of studying.

"No, it does not," Janey said, rescuing the dressing bottle. "It just means we'll take a longer lunch break and hit the books again when we get back."

Andy huffed and plopped a huge mound of mashed potatoes onto his plate.

"I'm going over in the morning to pick up my dog food," Dillon said. "I can deliver the box and make sure the place is still standing, if you'd like."

"Oh…well…" Something in Janey's tone set off a warning signal in Claire's head. "Claire can go with you then. She knows where the Warren place is."

The gravy boat slipped through Claire's fingers. She caught it just as a thick brown dollop landed on the table. Mumbling an apology, she mopped at the spot with her napkin while four pairs of eyes focused on her. But it was Dillon's that caught and held her attention. He wasn't smiling anymore. In fact, he looked uneasy, but about what or whom she couldn't be sure.

"I wouldn't want to impose," he said. "Claire must have more important things to do."

He spoke to Janey, yet his eyes never left Claire's. She got the unmistakable feeling he was daring her to disagree with him, and it piqued her curiosity. Her inborn compulsion to know why got the better of her.

"It's no problem," she said. "I'd be happy to show you around."

Darkness settled over Sommer Kennels like a velvet blanket shot through with bright points of light—clusters of them so low and thick Claire imagined she could reach up and grab a handful. She enjoyed this time of day, when the snow and the trees, the air itself, took on a quiet, wintry calm broken only by an occasional woof from the dog yard. Bundled in thick insulated pants and a heavy parka, she sat on the wide porch railing with her back to the house and gazed up at the sky, a mug of coffee cupped in her gloved hands to keep it from cooling too quickly. The rest of the family was inside watching TV. Judging by the light from the cookhouse, she assumed Dillon had settled in as well.

The dogs had been fed. It was a labor-intensive task that involved chopping up the ice that had formed in their pans and replacing it with a concoction of chicken, beef, and commercial dry dog food brewed in a cauldron of water over the woodstove in the cookhouse. It made for an unsightly soup, but the dogs devoured it with gusto. Ranger, named for the black Lone Ranger mask across his tan face, had slobbered across the toe of her boot to show his gratitude.

Claire thought of her dad in his tailored suits and how appalled he'd be if he knew what her day was like. She deliberately kept from him the more unglamorous details of her Alaskan adventure: cleaning kennels, the pervasive smell of dogs, being dragged behind an overturned sled. He didn't know about the sprained wrist and bruised tailbone she'd gotten running the Klondike 300 last year.

She often wondered what had attracted Ethan Stanfield to her mother, Caroline, a free spirit who had loved nature and getting her hands dirty, who had been more inclined to take their daughter on long hikes than to pay bills. Her dad tolerated the plants in the windowsills and merely shook his head the day he came home to find the backyard turned, one shovelful at a time, for a vegetable garden.

But he drew the line at having an animal in the house, so his reaction to Claire's desire to race sled dogs came as no surprise. "Have you lost your mind? You don't know anything about dogs."

It was true. When she first arrived, she hadn't been able to tell one from the other. Now, she couldn't imagine *not* being able to tell them apart. Like the Sommers, the dogs had become family. She wasn't a cheechako—a newcomer to Alaska—anymore.

"I'll learn," she told him.

She had been unable to explain the feelings that rushed through her when she flew over the Alaska Range for the first time or gazed up at the night sky as it swirled in a curtain of greens and blues. Nor could she explain the thrill she'd experienced at taking her first dogsled ride, the swoosh of plastic runners over packed snow, the rhythmic panting of the dogs as they clipped along, the air so cold it grabbed the breath from her lungs.

"How do I know you won't decide to stay up there?" her dad had asked. "You've worked hard to get where you are in the firm."

"And I won't abandon that," Claire replied. "But this is something I need to do for myself."

"Because of Grant?"

"No." She had let people believe Grant was her reason for accepting Janey's initial invitation to visit. The half-truth made a convenient excuse to get away for a while, put herself back together emotionally. But she asked for a leave of absence a month later because of the dogs. She hadn't gone to Alaska looking for love, but she had found it in a kennel yard of huskies. Their unconditional affection and tireless passion to run was infectious, the raw adventure of taking them across a wild, immense world of snow-covered mountains and frozen rivers irresistible.

"What if something happens up there, peanut?"

His softly voiced concern had brought tears to her eyes. She was eleven when her mama died of cancer. That was twenty years ago, yet her dad remained a widower. Locked in her own grief, Claire never questioned his choice. If she, his only child, didn't make it back, it would break his heart, along with the vow made by a scared little girl.

"I'll come home, Daddy. I promise."

Dillon stepped out of the house and saw Claire sitting under the porch light, her gaze unguarded against a backdrop of stars. He closed the door gently and watched for a moment—the curve of her mouth, the way her lips met the rim of the mug in her gloved hands. The craving returned and it annoyed him. The time and place were wrong. The woman was wrong. He figured it best to keep his distance, yet he found himself looking forward to spending time with her tomorrow.

He couldn't get to the cookhouse without being seen, so he stepped closer and said, "Beautiful night."

She flinched, sloshing the contents of her mug onto her parka. "Jeez, how long have you been standing there?"

"Not long." Dillon handed her the towel he'd intended to use to shave and leaned against the rail next to her. "Where were you just now?"

She wiped at the damp spot on her parka. "Thinking about my dad."

A memory of Dillon's own dad intruded—*you're not welcome in this house*—but he shoved it back into its dark space. "Is he the Stanfield, Wood, or...?" The last name escaped him.

"Keller," Claire said. "Dad's the Stanfield."

"What does that make you?"

She gave a soft laugh. "A long way from being a partner."

"Is that what you want? To be a law partner someday?"

Her whiskey eyes fixed on him, and Dillon felt like he'd downed a double shot.

"You say *law partner* like it's something you picked up on the bottom of your boot in the dog yard," she said.

He opened his mouth to deny the accusation, though it was closer to the truth than not.

"Never mind," she said, "I've heard the jokes comparing lawyers to dentists. Nobody likes them until they need one. When was the last time you saw a dentist?"

Dillon's thoughts were thrown sideways by her question. "It's been a while." And it had been a while since he'd sat in a witness box being grilled by a defense attorney. "Am I on trial?"

His question deflated her, and her shoulders sagged. "No, of course not." She puffed a long breath that sent a cloud of vapor skyward. "Guess I'm on edge after all that's happened today."

Dillon felt a tug at his conscience. He had his reasons for not wanting to talk about his past, but those reasons didn't have anything to do with this woman. "Your friends are good people, Claire. I shouldn't have embarrassed you in front of them earlier."

"Yes, well, I left myself open for it. I'll be more careful in the future."

He'd bet on that. "Janey doesn't miss a beat."

The comment brought a smile. "I warned you."

"I'll watch my step."

"I have the feeling you always do. Were you ever a cop?"

Dillon stilled. "What makes you ask?"

"The way you enter a room. The way you size people up. I have a feeling you don't miss much. I've worked with my share of police officers during my time in criminal defense."

"I fit the profile."

She caught the sarcasm in his voice and gave a dry chuckle. "I'm doing it again. Sorry." She slid to her feet and stood facing him.

She had more to say; he saw it in her eyes. He willed her to drop it, trying not to reveal the scabs her questions picked at. Her scrutiny left him feeling exposed. Then her expression relaxed, and he felt downright naked.

"I'm going inside," she said, "before I embarrass myself more than I already have. Breakfast is at seven. We feed the dogs at eight. I'd like to leave for the Warrens' as soon after that as possible."

"You don't have to go with me tomorrow."

She gave a snort that made him smile. "And stick around here so Janey can hound me about missed opportunities? No thanks."

Claire's brain refused to shut down as she lay in Andy's narrow bed and stared at the darkened ceiling. The rest of the family had gone to bed hours ago—Janey and Matt in their room at the end of the hall, and Andy on the front room couch. The red block numbers of the bedside clock—a replica of Mater from Disney's *Cars*—told her she should be asleep as well, but her conversation with Dillon on the porch had stirred a two-year-old memory, one she thought she had put behind her for good.

It was early evening and she had managed to get home early for the first time in weeks, had anticipated kicking her shoes off and fixing a nice dinner. Then she found the airline itinerary on the table: one way from Portland to New York; one seat reservation.

She looked up from the itinerary to the man she'd planned to share her home-cooked meal with. The man who, it turned out, had other plans. His dark-blond hair, longer than she'd ever seen it before, brushed the collar of his pastel-blue shirt. *When did he start wearing blue?* She thought he hated blue. *And when did he grow a chin strip?*

She held the itinerary out. "When were you going to tell me?"

He shrugged. "You haven't been around to talk. Even when you're here, your mind is on that case."

"I'm a defense attorney. It's what I do."

"It's all you do," he accused. "You've shut off your emotions. How else could you defend that monster and not feel anything?"

She felt too much—that was the problem. She locked herself in the bathroom to throw up in secret, took hot showers until her skin burned, downed an extra glass of wine at the end of the day to wash the taste of her client's crime out of her mouth. She thought it would be easier to deal with if she didn't talk about it, if she tried to maintain a semblance of normalcy at home.

"I didn't ask for this case, but I'm obligated to see it through to the end. I can't just pack up and walk away, like you appear ready to do."

"I've got work waiting for me in New York."

"Once the jury delivers—"

"I'm not hanging around that long." He grabbed the itinerary from her and stalked out of the room.

And later that evening, she watched him walk out of her life.

She'd told Dillon that nobody liked lawyers until they needed one. Grant had decided he no longer needed her.

Is that what you want? To be a law partner someday?

Dillon's question had annoyed her and she'd gone on the defensive, practically cross-examining him as a hostile witness, for God's sake. Then she'd made a lame attempt to excuse her behavior by laying the blame on Janey's match-making antics. But the real reason went much deeper.

Why now? Just when she had buried old hurts and regained her emotional balance, why did a man like Dillon Cord—who was too damn good looking and brought more questions than answers—have to show up?

Chapter 4

The following day dawned clear and sharp as Claire pulled onto the Warrens' property. Warming up the Land Cruiser had taken longer than the drive itself. Finding the place hardly required a guide, Dillon thought. He might have commented on Janey's apparent matchmaking scheme, but the strain in Claire's silence didn't invite conversation—she'd been about as prickly as a briar all morning. He figured it had something to do with their talk the night before but decided the less said, the better.

They got out of the four-wheel drive as a lanky teenager in a black snowsuit emerged from the cookhouse towing a cooler of steaming chow on a plastic sled. At the sight of the food, the fifty-or-more dogs in the kennel yard strained against their stake-out chains, their voices rising in a dissonance of short, eager barks and hungry woofs.

"All right, all right," the teen hollered above the noise. "I know you're hungry. I'm movin' as fast as I can."

"Good morning, Brian!" Claire called.

Brian Warren's scowl broke into a self-conscious grin. His narrow chest expanded. *I'll be damned,* Dillon thought, *the kid's got a thing for the lady lawyer.*

"Morning! I didn't hear you drive up."

Claire laughed and reached out to rub the ears of the first dog she came to, a black husky howling as if he hadn't eaten in weeks. "Gee, I wonder why!"

"Mingo, shut up," Brian ordered, but the dog had already quieted at Claire's attention.

"Brian, this is Dillon Cord, the musher from Nome," Claire said.

The teenager's expression tightened, as though he resented the intrusion on his territory. Dillon suppressed an amused smile. "Good to meet you." He didn't make an effort to shift the box of supplies in his arms so he could offer his hand and risk having it either ignored or crushed in a juvenile show of strength.

"Mr. Cord," Brian acknowledged. "Your bags of chow are in the back of the cookhouse."

"I appreciate that. Where would you like me to put this?"

Brian stepped forward and took the box from him. "I told Mrs. Sommer she didn't have to bother."

"Any news about your dad?" Claire asked.

"He'll be coming home tomorrow."

"That's wonderful." She put a hand on Brian's arm. "We all wish him the best."

The kid's face reddened. "Thanks."

Brian's awkward embarrassment reminded Dillon of unrequited crushes he'd had at that age. He almost felt sorry for the kid. "Looks like you could use some help," he remarked, taking in the size of the dog yard.

"I can handle it."

"I'm sure you can. But since we're here, why don't you let Claire put those things away and I'll clean kennels while you feed the dogs?"

He could tell the kid was surprised he'd offered to do the dirty work. Still, pride wouldn't allow him to accept the help too easily. Dillon gave what he hoped was a convincing smile and slapped his hands together as if he couldn't wait to shovel dog shit. "Where do you want me to start?"

Dillon offered to drive once his bags of dog chow had been loaded into the Land Cruiser. Claire tossed him the keys. "It was nice of you to help Brian," she said as they returned to Sommer Kennels.

"He's got a lot to manage by himself."

"Maybe Matt can get somebody from town to—"

"I told him I'd be back this evening."

"Oh. Good. That's good." Claire cringed. It was a way of life in such a remote area—people helping each other because there weren't many people around. Why did it surprise her that Dillon would offer to give Brian a hand?

He's not Grant, she told herself. *Stop comparing them.* She caught Dillon smiling. "What?"

"The kid's got a crush on you, counselor."

His nickname for her didn't go unnoticed, and she filed it away. "Don't be ridiculous. I'm old enough to be his mother… almost."

"Age doesn't mean anything when you're seventeen and a beautiful woman moves in next door."

The compliment skittered through her. Damn it, he was doing it again. She could pretend it had no effect on her and look like a fool, or she could acknowledge it and move on. "Thank you. But you're wrong about Brian. He's a polite, considerate—"

"Bundle of hormones. Has he asked you out yet?"

Claire felt a flush creep across her cheeks. "To a movie in Anchorage." She resented the defensiveness she could hear in her own voice. "Only because we both wanted to see the same movie. What?" she asked again, seeing his smirk.

"You aren't that naive."

No, she wasn't. She'd found a last-minute excuse to get out of going to the movie. In time, Brian's misguided feelings would be redirected toward someone closer to his own age. "I'm not about to encourage a teenager."

"And if he was twenty years older?"

"As I said yesterday, I'm not looking for a relationship." *You've shut off your emotions.* Grant's accusation echoed through Claire's thoughts like an icy wind.

"What if one finds you?"

Claire glanced over at him and wasn't at all pleased with the way her heart bumped against her ribcage when his gaze met hers. It was a harmless question, she told herself, but how could she really be sure what was going on behind those eyes that gave away nothing? And *harmless* didn't come close to describing her body's reaction to his presence. She looked away. "You're going to miss it."

"I didn't mean—"

"The turnoff," she interrupted. "You're going to miss the turnoff."

"Shit." He cranked the steering wheel, causing the dog chow in the back to shift, and narrowly made the end of the driveway in time. He brought the Land Cruiser to a stop at the cookhouse. "Sorry," he said, and gave a self-conscious laugh. "Guess I should have let you do the driving."

Claire turned to face him. "You were distracted," she said, more annoyed with herself than with him. "We both were," she admitted. "For everybody's safety, especially our dogs', let's agree to stay out of each other's way and focus on the upcoming race. Deal?"

He gave her a long, intent look with those unreadable eyes of his, then nodded. "You've got a deal." He glanced over at Janey working in the dog yard. "Your friend will be disappointed."

She's not the only one, Claire realized, troubled by the thought. "She'll get over it."

Chapter 5

Claire pulled the flaps of her bomber cap farther over her numbed cheeks, the smell of tanned leather and fur filling her frosted nostrils. Her flexed knees absorbed the trail's rough contours. The three-foot snow base had crusted overnight. Late morning sunlight bounced off icicles hanging from branches of spruce and birch. Attached to the gangline—a plastic-coated steel cable—in pairs spaced eight feet apart, her team followed the packed trail through the trees, their collars jingling in rhythm with their breath plumes.

"Hey, Handsome!" Claire shouted from the back of the sled. "How's my pretty boy doing up there?"

The black-and-white Alaskan husky running right lead

pricked his ears but didn't slow his steady trot. Claire smiled. She and Matt had chosen the five-year-old Iditarod veteran to lead her team out of Anchorage next Saturday. All the dogs looked healthy and ready. With only a week to go, she took them out in small groups for twenty-to-thirty-mile runs—just long enough to keep their muscles toned and interest high, but short enough that they'd feel rested before the race. Today she ran a team of eight.

The toboggan-style sled was loaded with four sixty-pound bags of dog food, but Claire wasn't lured into any false sense of control. Even with the added weight, if her four-legged powerhouses decided on another course, her only option would be to hold on. The first rule of dog sledding: don't let go of the sled. Over the past two years, she'd taken countless wild rides dragged behind a sled, but she had let go only once: the sinking feeling she experienced as the dogs and sled took off without her wasn't something she cared to repeat.

Except at meals and during kennel chores, she'd seen little of Dillon in the past forty-eight hours. That suited her fine, she told herself. Given all there was to do before the race, staying out of each other's way wasn't difficult. Food and gear destined for checkpoint drops along the trail had been shipped through the Iditarod Trail Committee Headquarters in Wasilla the week before. But mandatory and personal items for the sleds needed to be gathered and organized, the dogs' gear needed regular upkeep, and the dogs themselves needed to be taken for daily runs. True to his word, Dillon headed for the Warrens' place as soon as his own dogs were taken care of. Ted had come home from the hospital the previous afternoon but was still weak. Sarah had her hands full. That morning, Brian's friend had moved in short-term to help with chores, freeing Dillon to spend more time running his own dogs.

As predicted, Janey wasn't happy. She had cornered Claire in Andy's room after dinner the night before under the pretense of putting away folded laundry.

"It looks like the two of you are deliberately avoiding each other," she commented as she arranged an armload of rolled socks in the dresser drawer.

"Not at all." Claire hated lying to her friend—hated being put in a position where she felt the need to. "We've got a race to prep for."

"What about after the race?"

"You know the answer to that."

"I know you made a promise. But what does *Claire* want?" Janey lifted a silencing hand. "Just think about it, okay? And for heaven's sake, stop treating Dillon like he has a communicable disease." She frowned. "He doesn't, does he?"

Claire gave an incredulous laugh. "How should I know?"

That was the problem. She didn't know anything about the man, other than his apparent distaste for lawyers. She could respect his secrets, but she didn't have to like them. Nor did she have to like the way he seemed to creep into her thoughts when she let her guard down.

Her team approached a fork in the trail. "Gee, Handsome! Treker, gee!" The husky leaders tugged in their nylon harnesses and took the right fork. Swing dogs Toolik and Ranger—responsible for cornering and keeping the gangline stretched out—followed suit, along with Pepper and Trouble. Moments later, the lead dogs dropped out of sight. The sled rushed through the trees as if pulled by an invisible force, and Claire's pulse tripped with excitement. Tightening her grip on the handlebar, she leaned into the turn.

The trail straightened and the head of her team reappeared. An instant later, she saw Daisy, running right wheel position in front of the sled's brush bow, raise her tail. Sugar, running left wheel, followed suit. The solid-white husky sisters were usually too modest for such a display unless they sensed something out of the ordinary. Claire ran her eyes over the length of her team and realized every one of the eight dogs was on alert, their strides sharp. Eight pairs of ears tilted forward.

Claire's heart accelerated as she scanned the trail ahead. There had been very few run-ins with moose this winter, but the danger was always present. Aggressive toward dogs, and often tired and hungry, moose would do their best to kill an entire team rather than give up the trail. Cows with calves were especially dangerous. Claire felt for Matt's .357 Magnum revolver in the small bag beneath the handlebar. He'd insisted she learn to use the handgun and carry it whenever she took the dogs out. The idea of shooting at a living creature made her stomach churn, but when it came to defending her dogs, she liked to think she would do it without hesitation. And she was an accurate shot.

Her dogs followed a bend in the trail and Claire rode the drag between the runners, hoping not to crash into an eight-hundred-pound protective mother waiting for them around the corner.

Relief flooded through her as the trail straightened. Instead of a moose, she saw Dillon and his team, who had been coming from the opposite direction and had pulled off the trail. An instant later, she realized one of his dogs was tangled. Dillon was struggling through the deep snow to reach a husky whose neck line had become wrapped around a thick bush.

Claire stood on the brake bar. "Whoa!" Her team stopped and she yanked the snow hook from its carrier and stomped it into the trail's crust.

"I need slack on the gangline!" Dillon shouted. He'd reached his dog but was having trouble finding the neck line in the brush. The dog jerked and whipped its head to free itself, compounding the problem.

Claire grabbed the gangline ahead of the trapped dog and pulled. The rest of the team seemed to think it was some sort of game and pulled back; the harder she pulled, the harder they pulled. She glanced back and saw the desperation on Dillon's face. His dog was choking.

"Whoa, you bozos!" she cried in frustration, no match for their combined strength. "Please stop!"

The gangline abruptly went slack, sending Claire backward onto her butt in the snow.

Dillon freed his tangled dog—a broad-chested black-and-white Alaskan husky—and checked him for injuries. The dog licked his face repeatedly, showing his gratitude.

Claire picked herself up and brushed the snow off her backside. She watched as Dillon secured the rescued dog, then made his way down the line. "Come on, Blackie," he said as he lifted a blue-eyed jet-black husky off its feet, "up and over." He set the dog down on the other side of the gangline. "I know we don't have any trees at home, Chevron," he said to the next dog, who had somehow wrapped its tug line around a small spruce, "but you can't take this one with you." He unsnapped the line, worked the twist out, and reattached it to the dog's harness.

Again, Claire was moved by the compassion and patience Dillon showed his team. When he was with his dogs, he let his defenses down—no inscrutable looks or guarded secrets. It was a side of him she found herself drawn to. She helped him lead his team back onto the trail behind her sled. His hands were unsteady as he retrieved his gloves from the snow and pulled them over his reddened fingers. "Are you all right?" she asked.

He gave a half smile. "Bozos?"

She chuckled. "It was the only thing I could think of at the time." Then her mood sobered. "I'm sorry, Dillon."

He looked surprised. "For what?"

"If I hadn't talked you into making that stupid deal, we would have sat down together and planned our routes to prevent something like this from happening."

"In that case, I'm just as much to blame." He smirked. "I didn't have to agree to the stupid deal."

Claire appreciated his attempt to make light of the situation, but his dogs could have been seriously injured. Hers as well. "Why did you?" she asked.

He studied her a moment. Then his eyes narrowed and he said, "Because you were right, counselor. We need to stay focused on the race."

"Yes, we do." She drew a cold, sharp breath through her teeth and plunged on, determined to get at the truth. "So what was it? You get one too many traffic tickets? Is that why my being an attorney bothers you?"

His gaze became brittle. "You remind me of things I left behind. Things I'm not going to talk about."

Finally, an honest answer. Though she would have preferred he talk about it, Claire chose not to press her luck. "As long as you agree I'm not responsible."

"You're not responsible."

"Good," she said. "No more smart-ass remarks about lawyers, all right? And no more calling me *counselor* like it's a dirty word."

The tension in his expression eased. If she hadn't known better, she would have said he almost wanted to smile. "No more smart-ass remarks."

Claire heard a scuffle behind her and turned to see Trouble snap at Pepper. "Knock it off!" Returning her attention to Dillon, she said, "They're getting restless. I should go before they decide to finish the run without me." She fixed him with a level look. "Are we okay, you and me?"

"We're okay. Thanks again for your help."

He gave in to his smile then, and Claire had to suck air back into her lungs before replying. "You're welcome."

Her dogs yipped and danced, eager to go. She was too. *Okay* didn't begin to describe the feelings ricocheting through her. Putting distance between herself and the man who was causing those feelings seemed like the smart thing to do. She grabbed her sled's handlebar and pulled up the hook. "Let's go!" she called, and her team lunged into action.

Dillon watched Claire and her dogs cruise around the bend and disappear from sight. His dogs whined and bit at the snow, wanting to follow. "Settle down." He identified with their desire, felt it pulse through him. He found himself thinking about Claire with annoying frequency. He couldn't ignore it any more than he seemed to be able to stay out of her way.

Dillon had the feeling she was damn good at her job: examining evidence, asking the right questions, making deals. It was a tightrope act being near her and keeping his past where it belonged. Buried. But Claire wasn't the enemy. She had come to his rescue in Talkeetna, and today her quick action may well have saved Dodge's life. His dogs weren't conditioned for these kinds of trails. Claire was right—they should have mapped out their routes beforehand instead of avoiding each other. Smart-ass remarks? Hell, he'd been acting like some snot-nosed kid, blaming her for his own failures.

No, she wasn't the problem. He was. He needed to keep his head in the game, focus on getting his dogs ready for the race, and stop allowing his thoughts to dwell on a past he couldn't undo. But he felt the encroachment of a long-suppressed claustrophobia that had nothing to do with sled-busting trees, and it worried the shit out of him.

Chapter 6

Claire fit Andy and the squirming four-month-old puppy in the digital camera's display while five other tricolored bundles tumbled over the toes of her boots. The litter of Alaskan huskies, sired by Handsome, bounced and rolled over each other as they vied for attention.

"Say cheese!" Claire called over the pups' yips and adolescent barks.

"Chee—yuck!" Andy sputtered as the pup he'd named Noel licked him on the mouth.

Containing a laugh, Claire took the picture. "One more before you have to go in for lessons."

"Okay." Andy struggled to maintain his hold on the squirming puppy. "Hey, Dillon!"

"Hey, sport!"

Claire nearly dropped the camera at the sound of Dillon's voice close behind her. She turned and saw him standing an arm's length away, his dark-green snow bibs hanging loose over a black turtleneck. He looked tired, and his brown hair was tousled, as if he'd run his fingers through it in place of a comb. Claire had heard him take a team out after everyone went to bed the night before, then heard him return hours later, yet he'd been up and helping with the dogs by eight in the morning. Tired looked good on him, she decided.

His easy smile made her pulse hum. "Nice camera," he said.

"Her old boyfriend gave it to her," Andy informed him.

Claire cringed. "I don't think Dillon wants to hear about that, hon."

Andy didn't take the hint. "Auntie Claire came to visit us after he dumped her. She called him a big mistake and cried and threw things."

"No kidding."

Claire closed her eyes and groaned.

"His name was Hammertown and—"

"Hamilton," Claire corrected. "Grant Hamilton."

"Yeah, and he—"

"Andrew Sommer!" Janey called from the cabin porch. "Lunch break's over! Time for math!"

Andy sighed and put Noel on the ground to rejoin her brothers and sisters. "Don't forget you're gonna teach me how to play poker tonight," he said to Dillon on his way out of the pen.

"I won't forget."

"Poker?" Claire asked.

"He wants me to play a game with him and it's the only one I know. Will his folks object?"

"They'll probably ask to be dealt in." Maybe she'd invite herself to a place at the table too. "Andy's really taken a liking to you."

"The feeling's mutual."

A blue-eyed puppy named Joy wobbled over and nosed at Dillon's boot. Claire knelt and took the pup's picture. Straightening, she looked at the camera in her hand. Dillon had been honest with her; she could do the same. "This is one of the few things Grant didn't take with him when he moved to New York."

"New York?"

She found the derision in his voice surprisingly satisfying. "He said he had a job offer, but..." She let her voice trail off.

"He didn't ask you to go with him?"

"He knew I wouldn't. I used to think that was why he chose the East Coast: it was as far from Portland as he could get without leaving the country." It felt good to be able to say it without the bitterness that used to stick in her throat.

"And now?"

"Now it doesn't matter. *He* doesn't matter. I got a nice camera and one hell of a vacation out of the deal."

Dillon didn't ask what had led to their breakup, but Claire felt the question hanging in the air. She wanted to talk about it, she realized, wanted him to understand. "I had this case, a client facing the death penalty. The media had him convicted before the trial even began. Grant couldn't accept that I was representing such an obviously guilty man, that I'd stay late at the office, that I'd miss dinner dates. He accused me of being more in love with my work than with him."

She expected Dillon to ask her if Grant's accusation was true—something she'd asked herself countless times in the past two years. If she answered honestly, she'd have to say yes. She wondered now how much she'd ever really loved the man she'd lived with. She knew she didn't miss him.

Instead, Dillon said, "My wife used to accuse me of the same thing." At Claire's stunned silence, he explained, "Ex-wife. We divorced seven years ago."

Somehow the possibility of an ex–Mrs. Dillon Cord hadn't entered Claire's mind. It made her wonder if he had—

"Children?" Horrified that she'd said it aloud, she stammered, "I'm sorry, that's none of my business."

"It's all right," he said. "No, I don't have children."

Claire couldn't tell if he was relieved or saddened by that fact. She longed to ask what line of work he'd been in at the time of his divorce. But she had promised herself to shelve the probing attorney for a while and not push the man for answers. *Who knows? I might even give soft and vulnerable a shot,* she mused, then resisted the impulse to laugh at the thought.

As they moved to leave the puppy pen, she said, "Looks like we have more in common than just the Iditarod."

He gave that slanted smile she found too attractive. "Looks that way."

From the corner of her eye, Claire saw Noel make a dash for the open gate. As she jumped back to cut off the pup's escape, she bumped square into Dillon. The unexpected contact sent a tingle through her.

Okay, maybe soft and vulnerable wasn't all that impossible. Uncomfortable with the realization, she took a retreating step toward the cabin. "Well, I still have a bazillion dog booties to sew." Not entirely true—most of the booties had shipped to checkpoints last week—but it was the best she could come up with in the moment. She took another step. "I'll see you at dinner."

"What happened to the client facing death?"

She stopped and drew in a shallow breath. The familiar knot tightened in her stomach. "He got life with the possibility of parole."

"A small victory then."

"He deserved worse."

Dillon's brow lifted a fraction. "You were his defense attorney."

"It doesn't mean I had to like him." She couldn't bring herself to say the man's name—wouldn't allow it to stain her lips. "That was one of the tough ones."

"Could you have gotten him acquitted?"

"No. He beat a couple and their two young children to death." The photos of the bludgeoned three-year-old girl would haunt her for the rest of her life. She wished to God she could have gotten justice for the murdered family. She wished to God she hadn't been so good at her job that time.

"And you took the case."

Claire stared at Dillon for long seconds, surprised he'd picked up on her deep-rooted regret so easily. "Yes," she said, and walked away.

Chapter 7

Dillon could only be thankful he hadn't acted on his impulse to dare her to a round of strip poker after everyone else had gone to bed. He'd be freezing his naked butt off by now while she sat across from him, comfortable in her pink sweats, giving him that damn Cheshire grin.

"Another hand?" Claire asked, raking the cards into a pile in front of her.

"Yes." They kept their voices low to avoid waking Andy, who had fallen asleep on the couch at the other end of the room. Janey and Matt had tossed in their cards a short while after.

"You haven't got any matchsticks left."

"Extend my credit."

"You're already in the hole for two hundred."

Dillon feigned irritation, enjoying the camaraderie they'd slid into. He knew how much it had cost her to talk about the murder case earlier, saw in her eyes how deep the scar went. She'd been closer to the truth than she realized when she said they had more in common than the upcoming race. "Afraid my luck's going to change?"

Her grin widened. "Fifty okay?"

"Fifty's fine."

She counted matches from her stock, made a notation on the pad next to her, and slid the pile across the table. "You don't like losing, do you?" she asked as she shuffled the cards.

"You cheated."

"Did not." She finished shuffling—her long fingers with their blunt nails never missing a beat—and placed the stack in the center of the table.

"You pretended not to understand the game when Andy and his folks were playing with us." Dillon cut the cards.

Claire began dealing. "I asked questions I thought would help Andy pick up on the game quicker. That's not cheating."

"You played dirty then."

She gave a low laugh and tossed in her ante. "There's no law against that."

"There ought to be."

And there ought to be a law against the way she made him feel when she laughed. Much of her honey-blond hair had come loose from the braid at the back of her head. It framed her face, giving her a disheveled look. His lack of concentration on the game didn't surprise him.

He tossed a matchstick in with hers and picked up the cards she'd dealt him. He tossed ten more matches into the pile. "Give me two."

Claire met his bet and took three cards for herself. "You give yourself away when you do that."

"Do what?"

"Tap your heel."

Dillon's foot froze midtap. "Anything else?"

"The left corner of your mouth twitches."

"I'll keep that in mind. Play cards."

He won that hand and the next, then lost four straight. Claire laid down a full house, beating his three aces. He uttered a disgusted curse, genuine and colorful.

She added her winnings to the pile of matches on her side. "You didn't think I'd give away all my secrets, did you?"

It had crossed his mind. "You can't tell me you aren't dealing off the bottom."

"A lawyer's greatest asset is her ability to read people."

"What was I doing this time?"

"Nothing."

"You just said—"

"You started to tap your heel, then caught yourself and stopped. You reached up to scratch your jaw, then stopped. Frankly, you were making me nervous with all your fidgeting."

"Deal the cards." Within minutes, he lost two more hands and the last of his matches. He tossed in his cards. "I give."

"How about some hot chocolate?"

"Trying to soothe my wounded ego?"

She gave a soft laugh. "Not really. I was going to fix myself some and thought it only polite to offer."

"Hot chocolate sounds good."

Claire heated two mugs of milk in the microwave while Dillon found the chocolate mix and spoons. The edginess returned. He felt it like a live electrical wire stretched across the room between them. Standing next to her at the counter, he watched her pour a packet of chocolate into each mug.

"You're trembling," he softly observed.

Her spoon clattered against the rim of her mug. He couldn't read her face because she held her head tipped away from him. "I haven't been sleeping well," she said, a tightness in her voice that hadn't been there a minute ago. "I guess the race being so close has made me jumpy."

Dillon figured her comment was a diversion and played along. "Did you get your booties done?"

"Only half a bazillion more to go."

He raised his mug in a toast. "Here's to dog booties."

"To dog booties." She touched the rim of her mug to his and took a cautious sip.

Dillon did the same. Once she lowered her mug, he took it from her and set it on the counter next to his own. Her eyes, wide and too damn vulnerable, met his. He slid an arm around her waist and coaxed her to him. She was slender beneath her chunky sweatshirt, but not fragile. He imagined the feel of her long legs wrapped around him. He risked brushing his lips over her cheek and heard her breath catch.

Claire thought she'd be ready for the impact. She was wrong. Her knees felt like she'd stepped backward off the runners of a speeding sled. The taste of chocolate enticed her as his tongue persuaded her to let him in. She did. His hand at her back pressed her closer. Their difference in size, the way their contrasting shapes fit together, the smell of him toyed with her balance. She sank her fingers into his hair as his mouth took her breath.

He cupped his hand around her butt and pulled her deeper into him. What little breath Claire still possessed escaped in a rush. *I'm lost*, she thought as her body craved more.

"Gross!"

Claire tore her mouth from Dillon's. Andy stood at the edge of the light from the kitchen, his Transformer pajamas rumpled and a look on his face like he had a mouth full of cooked cauliflower. She met the latent desire in Dillon's eyes as his heart beat a wild rhythm she felt through his entire body. He gave a half smile of regret and looked past her to Andy. "Did we wake you, sport?"

"I smelled hot chocolate."

Claire leaned into Dillon a moment longer, her equilibrium not yet stable. She felt his lips against her hair. "Did we just run to Nome?" he whispered.

She smiled into the side of his neck. "I think so." She pulled herself out of his arms, smoothed the front of her sweatshirt where it had ridden up, and turned to face Andy. "Sit at the table, hon. I'll fix you a mug."

"Are you guys finished kissing?" he asked, unconvinced.

Claire shot Dillon a quick, self-conscious glance.

The unguarded look he gave her sent heat to her cheeks. Ignoring the boy, he pushed her hair back and tucked it behind her ear, his calloused fingers gentle.

And not quite steady. The kiss had shaken him as much as it had her. Claire felt a tug of panic. She was afraid the relationship she'd said she wasn't looking for was standing right in front of her. "I'll get that hot chocolate."

Chapter 8

From the back of the crowded Dena'ina Center's banquet hall, Claire tried to focus on the veteran musher onstage recounting an experience he'd had during last year's Iditarod, but she was unable to hear anything over the dull roar in her ears. She couldn't seem to draw enough air into her lungs to shake off the blackness moving in on her peripheral vision.

So light-headed...

The room tipped and the black curtains drew together over her eyes. A strong arm encircled her waist and kept her from diving to the floor.

"Let's get out of here." Dillon's breath brushed her ear.

Claire nodded. He grabbed their coats and guided her out

to the parking lot. Bracing herself against the side of the Land Cruiser, Claire gulped the crisp night air and felt her head clear.

"Better?"

"Yes. Thanks." She gave a self-conscious laugh and rubbed her arms. "I don't know what came over me."

Dillon helped her into her parka. "Too much excitement, too little sleep. I'm having the same problem."

She cast him a skeptical look. "Seriously?"

He shrugged into his own parka. "Seriously."

"I just thought since you'd done this before—"

"I'd be used to it?" He leaned against the side of the Land Cruiser, his shoulder pressed to hers. "If anything, it's worse. I've been there. I know what to expect. Happy River, Dalzell Gorge, the Buffalo Tunnels. I almost scratched at Kaltag my first year. The wind and cold on the Yukon were brutal."

"Then why keep coming back?"

He looked up at the night sky; Claire looked at him. It was easy to do.

"There's a raw beauty on the Iditarod Trail you won't find anywhere else. You'll discover what you're made of." When he looked back at her, the intensity in his eyes made her heart quicken. "And you'll never be the same when it's over."

She felt it even now. After spending so much time working with the dogs and absorbing the unique culture and spirit of Alaska, she was already changed. Alaska had gotten into her blood.

And so had this man. She knew too little about him—only that he had a past he refused to discuss and an ex-wife who had resented his job, whatever that job may have been. Claire didn't like secrets, especially the kind that might pop up and bite her when least expected. There'd been an awkward silence between them since the night of the poker game. She had no clue as to his thoughts.

But she could still taste his kiss.

A shiver ran through her and she glanced away.

"You're cold," he said. "Let's get in."

Claire felt time press down on her as she gazed out the passenger window at the waning moon. She'd heard Iditarod nights were the worst: bitter winds, incredible loneliness, cold intense enough to freeze alcohol. In the past few days, there'd been little time to worry about it. Just as there'd been little time to dwell on the kiss and its implications—whatever those may be. The day before had been devoted to the pre-race veterinary check at Iditarod Headquarters in Wasilla. Brian had brought the Warren truck over to help Dillon transport his team, while Claire and Matt loaded her team in the Sommers' truck. The dogs were examined, wormed, and given health certificates, along with proof of vaccinations and microchip IDs.

Then, early this morning, she and Dillon drove the hundred miles to Anchorage to attend the mandatory mushers' meeting: a chaotic assembly of rookies and veterans, officials laying out rules and veterinarians speaking on dog care. Much of it was a rehash of information Claire already knew, and she found it difficult to stay focused. The whole affair had gone on for hours, with a midday break for pictures with their IditaRiders. As part of an annual fundraiser auction, a fifty-eight-year-old doctor from Texas had entered the highest bid for the privilege of racing the first eleven miles of the Iditarod with Claire. She only hoped she didn't dump him out of the sled on the first sharp turn. Dillon's IditaRider was a mother of three from Fairbanks.

The banquet began at 6:00 p.m. Mushers dined on

boneless beef ribs and drew for their starting positions. Out of almost seventy participants, Claire would be the twenty-second musher to leave Anchorage on Saturday morning. Dillon drew number eighteen.

Saturday morning. The day after tomorrow. Claire felt green in more ways than one. Nerves churned the contents of her stomach; she'd come close to fainting, for God's sake. She cast Dillon a look from the corner of her eye. The Land Cruiser's dash lights shadowed the angles of his face, sharpening his features. He drove with both hands on the steering wheel. Strong hands. Her body suffused with heat as she remembered their heart-stopping tenderness.

"You all right?" he asked.

The intimacy in his voice only intensified the heat. She cleared her throat. "I'm fine. Did you get your shopping done this afternoon?"

"Yeah." He pulled a small paper bag from a pocket of his parka and tossed it into her lap.

She looked inside. "A box of matches?"

"I always pay my debts."

"There's three hundred here. The debt was only two-fifty."

"Interest."

"Twenty percent? Steep. Generous, but steep." Claire put the matches in her pocket. "About the other day—"

"I don't regret it."

She stared at him and felt her face grow warm as she realized he was referring to the kiss. "Nor do I," she admitted.

"But that's not what you wanted to talk about, is it?"

"I..." She tucked her hair behind her ear. "No." *That doesn't mean I haven't thought about it,* she wanted to tell him, but fear held her back. The emotions were still too raw, too uncertain.

"What is it, Claire?"

"When I told you about the murder trial, how did you know?" she asked. Seeing his confused look, she added, "That I regretted taking the case."

"It's how I would have felt—the need to avenge the innocent. It eats at you."

Yes. It ate at her. It haunted her in spite of all the well-meaning advice she had received. *Don't personalize the case, Claire. This is your job. Let it go and move on.*

"Will you go back to it when this is over?" Dillon asked.

A lump lodged in Claire's throat. She honestly didn't know. She'd return to Portland, of course, but would she be ready to practice law again? The longer she stayed in Alaska, the less the thought appealed to her. "I made a promise to my dad," she said by way of an answer.

"To come back to the law firm?"

"To come home."

The night sky shimmered to life, becoming a curtain of greens that swirled and waved like colored sheets hanging from the line on laundry day. Dillon pulled to the side of the road and stopped. He left the engine running, the heater fan blowing warmth across their faces. The green waves of light shifted direction, took on a reddish hue at the edges.

"I never get tired of seeing that," Claire whispered, as though saying it too loud might frighten it away.

"The first time I saw the northern lights, I was on some back road, lost, trying to read an Anchorage city map." He grinned, the lights turning his teeth an eerie green. "I was a cab driver at the time."

Claire burst out laughing.

"I didn't have the job very long. Then I took a job selling snow machines, but I sucked at sales." He paused, as though withdrawing into a memory. His smile flattened. "The only thing I was ever good at was being a cop," he said in a subdued voice. "But I fucked that up too."

While Claire grappled for a response, the northern lights faded and Dillon put the Land Cruiser in gear. The hard set of his profile didn't encourage questions. He'd closed himself off again. It was evident he hadn't intended to reveal as much as he had, that if he could take it back, he would in a heartbeat.

She'd guessed right about the cop part. That it hadn't worked out for him could mean just about anything. Maybe it had something to do with avenging the innocent, as he put it. At least now she understood why she reminded him of things he didn't want to talk about. The two professions relied on each other to uphold the law, often from opposite sides of a case. She'd butted heads with her share of disgruntled officers over legal issues, especially when she'd gotten between them and a confession.

"So," she said, remembering her vow not to grill him for details, "given your habit of fucking things up, should I avoid eating at the Bering West when I get to Nome?"

His startled laugh released the tension between them. "You're safe," he told her. "I've got an outstanding cook."

It was almost midnight when Dillon pulled into Sommer Kennels. He shut off the Land Cruiser's engine and Claire's head popped up beside him. She frowned as if disoriented, then yawned wide.

"Sorry. I must have dozed off."

Dillon saw no reason to inform her she'd begun snoring ten minutes after he opened his big mouth about being a cop. He was grateful she hadn't asked the questions he'd seen in her face at the revelation. "Sleep while you can," he said. "There won't be much time for it on the trail."

"So I hear. Thanks." She fumbled the door open, muttered good night, and headed for the cabin.

In less than thirty hours, they'd repeat the hundred-mile drive to Anchorage with loaded dog trucks for the start of the race. Dillon planned to use the Warren truck again to transport his team. Brian had agreed to be his handler for both the ceremonial start in Anchorage on Saturday morning and the restart in Willow on Sunday afternoon. From that point on, the mushers and their teams would be on official race time: run, rest, feed, check feet, repeat. It would be an endless cycle until reality shifted and time ceased to matter.

Cold, exhaustion, incredible beauty, numbing routine, and the dogs. Always the dogs. He wouldn't be here if not for them. They didn't ask questions. They didn't judge. They trusted unconditionally.

They kept him sober.

Instead of going to the cookhouse, he headed for the kennel yard. He was tempted to take a small team out for a night run but decided against it; the danger of an injury this close to the race was too risky. Bonnie dozed on a bed of straw in front of her shelter, her tail curled over her nose for warmth. She raised her ears at his approach. He knelt beside her and massaged her shoulders.

"Are you ready to do this again?" he asked, keeping his voice low.

She rolled onto her back for a belly rub. Dillon obliged. This would be her second Iditarod with him, and her fourth overall. She had previously belonged to a man who wandered into the Bering West three years ago in need of money. He couldn't afford to keep his kennel anymore, he said, and it broke his heart to have to sell his dogs. Dillon bought Bonnie and Clyde and got the story behind their names. Frank Johnson, who was tending bar that day, bought Guy more out of sympathy for the dog than any charity toward the distraught man. "A dog that dopey needs all the sympathy it can get," Frank reasoned. To everybody's surprise, what the hound lacked in smarts he made up for in pulling power. Except for Bonnie and Clyde, all of Dillon's Iditarod team this year came from Frank's kennel.

Dillon went to each member of his team, talked to them, gave them massages and belly rubs. Elliot popped to his feet and shook, ready to go. Dillon chuckled. "Easy, little man. It's not time yet."

It didn't take the dogs long to settle back to sleep, the rookies taking their cue from the veterans. But Dillon knew there would be no sleep for him tonight. Sleep left him vulnerable. The only way to ensure the past stayed where it belonged was to occupy his mind with the present. He still had harnesses to mend. He'd start there.

Chapter 9

The next day became a blur of checking and rechecking gear to pack in the sled: a five-gallon cooler to store dog food, sixteen dog dishes, a three-gallon alcohol cooker, spare bottles of HEET fuel for non-checkpoint stops, matches and more matches, headlamps, batteries and more batteries, gloves and liners, chemical hand warmers, a cold-weather sleeping bag, snowshoes, a first aid kit, extra socks, long johns, goggles…the list went on and on. Claire had done her homework and understood the importance of being ready for anything and everything. She saw little of Dillon. It was just as well. She needed to stay focused on every detail, and that seemed impossible when he was nearby.

She called her dad in the evening, catching him at the office. He answered on the second ring. "Ethan Stanfield."

Hearing his familiar voice always made her feel ten years old again. "Hi, Daddy."

"Peanut, how are you?"

She sat on the edge of Andy's bed and gave an unsteady laugh. Her stomach was in a constant state of turmoil, and her mind refused to shut down at the end of the day. As Dillon had put it, too much excitement, too little sleep. "The race begins in the morning. I feel like I'm going into court for the first time," she told her dad.

"Court's a hell of a lot safer."

"Not necessarily." She remembered her first jury trial, the nervous sweat, the shaking hands, the high-pitched voice that broke embarrassingly. She'd been terrified of forgetting her own client's name. What was a thousand miles of snow and ice in comparison? "Are you signed up to follow my progress on the Iditarod's website?"

"Maggie tells me I'm signed up and bookmarked."

Claire smiled and secretly thanked Maggie. "The beginning of the race will be broadcast live online, too, so you can watch me leave Anchorage. Look for bib twenty-two."

"Twenty-two. Got it." She heard the scratch of his pen. "There's no talking you out of this insanity?"

"Dad—"

"Forget I said that. I'm just an old man who misses his daughter."

"You could meet me in Nome at the end of the race," she offered, already knowing his answer. He hadn't visited her once. An aversion to cold, he said. If she hadn't flown home for Christmases, she wouldn't have seen him at all during her stay in Alaska.

"I'd rather have you home," he replied. Claire felt a lump swell in her throat. "Be safe out there, peanut."

"I will." She blinked away tears and attempted to lighten the mood. "God knows I'm hauling enough gear to survive a small apocalypse."

"Is that supposed to make me feel better?"

She gave a tired laugh. "Sorry. I should get back to inventorying all this stuff. I promise I'll call when I reach Nome."

"I'll be waiting."

She ended the call and looked up. Dillon stood in the doorway, wearing a fresh pair of jeans and a blue flannel shirt, his wet hair slicked back and his grooming kit in hand. "The shower's free," he said.

She felt an unexpected frisson at the thought of him bathing in the next room. Naked. "Thanks."

"Did you reach your dad?"

"Yes. He's worried about me."

"You're lucky."

The softness in his voice squeezed her heart. "Do you have somebody," she asked, "family somewhere, worrying about you?"

"Not anymore." Harsher this time. Another off-limits topic. "We've got an early morning ahead of us. Try to get some rest." He made to move from the doorway.

"Dillon?"

He paused, his eyes settling on her. That shiver of attraction coursed through Claire again, undeniable and too strong to ignore. She tossed her phone onto the bed and crossed the room, stopping only when she was certain he could hear the rush of her pulse. "In case there isn't a chance tomorrow," she said, and kissed him.

He tasted of mint toothpaste, his mouth welcoming and

gentle. He wrapped his free arm around her waist and closed the space between them until she could no longer distinguish her heartbeat from his. Her equilibrium tilted. She felt unguarded tenderness in the way he held her, needed her.

She kissed him until her tears threatened to return. Drawing back, she caressed his smooth-shaven cheek and whispered, "See you in Nome."

"That's a promise."

Chapter 10

They arrived in Anchorage before dawn. Matt drove, and Janey, Andy, and Claire squeezed beside him on the Ford's bench seat. Following the taillights of the Warren truck, they made their way to the staging area, where race officials directed them to their assigned parking spots along Fourth Avenue and side streets. Claire recognized some of the big names in sled dog racing, their handlers performing like well-trained pit crews, their trucks and trailers sporting logos of major pet food producers, banks, and airlines. Her lone sponsor was the law firm, with a huge chunk of her own savings tossed in.

Crowds gathered along the snow fences on each side

of the street, a festive mix of furs and wolf-head hats contrasting with the latest high-tech all-weather gear in a variety of neon colors. Photographers and video crews chose their positions to set up, preparing to record each musher and team as they left Anchorage. City officials had trucked in snow and spread it on a roadway that they worked to keep clear the rest of the year. The Chugach Mountains appeared to block the east end of Fourth Avenue, the ascending sun backlighting their imposing ridgeline.

The air vibrated with excited barking and keening howls. Claire felt her team stir in the back, their restlessness causing the truck to sway on its springs. Her stomach rolled, uneasy with the back-and-forth motion. She'd been unable to get more than a couple hours of sleep, mentally packing and repacking her sled once her head hit the pillow. Fueled by adrenaline and the caffeine Janey had pumped into her, Claire focused on one goal: to get out of Anchorage without embarrassing herself.

Dillon had looked as ragged as she felt when he grabbed his coffee and inhaled a bowl of oatmeal earlier that morning. When Brian and John pulled up in the Warren truck, he downed the last of his coffee, shot Claire a wink, and stumbled out to load his gear and dogs.

"Over there," Janey said, breaking into Claire's thoughts.

Matt pulled into the space reserved for team twenty-two and killed the engine. "Are you ready for this?" he asked with way too much cheer for Claire's jangled nerves.

She attempted a smile but suspected it looked closer to a grimace. She'd been wrong, she decided, as her breakfast threatened to come up. This *was* worse than facing a jury trial for the first time.

Brian and his friend John helped Dillon run stake-out chains along each side of the Warren truck. The dogs came out in the order in which they would be harnessed, starting with Bonnie. She sniffed the air as Dillon lifted her from the compartment, her body trembling with anticipation. "This is it, girl," he said, and clipped her to the lead at the front of the truck.

Maverick came out next. The lean Alaskan husky, named after the popular *Top Gun* character thanks to his speed, would run lead with Bonnie. Dillon paired the dogs by their personalities. Mild-tempered Chevron—black with a white inverted v on his chest—would run swing with his brother Blackie. Rocky, Clyde, Deshka, and Stewie—a resilient, tall malamute—made up the core team and were unloaded in that order. Three-year-old Windy, a brown-eyed husky who loved to please, licked Dillon's face at every opportunity as she was being unloaded. Gretchen, another eager-to-please husky, followed suit. The two females looked identical but for the scar on Gretchen's nose, put there by Dodge when she had gotten too close to his food dish.

Due to the crowds and the challenges of maneuvering through downtown city streets, Dillon chose to begin the race with only twelve dogs in harness. That just left his wheel dogs to unload. Because they were first to feel the weight of the sled when the team started out, the wheel position usually went to the largest dogs. Max, another tall, powerful malamute, would run left wheel. Last out of the truck was Guy, Dillon's strongest puller. Too laid back to be bothered by the constant noise of the sled runners close behind him, Guy was perfect for right wheel position.

Controlling even a reduced team on the first day of a race could be nearly impossible. The dogs were fresh and eager to run, howling and lunging in their harnesses to chase the teams ahead of them, stirred to a fever pitch by the noise and enthusiasm of spectators leaning over the snow fences on either side. A handler driving a tag sled—a smaller sprinter sled towed behind the musher's sled—was required for the first eleven miles to the Campbell Airstrip checkpoint, not only to add extra weight and braking power but also to help straighten out tangles. Brian had volunteered to drive the tag sled.

"You'll be doing most of the braking," Dillon stressed. "I don't want you rear-ending me."

"Got it."

The kid said he'd handled for other mushers, including his dad, who ran the Iditarod two years prior, but Dillon didn't want to leave anything to chance. During his first Iditarod, his tag sled driver—a last-minute replacement for a sick friend—panicked and bailed at the sight of a small birch coming at her. The driverless sled smashed into the tree, shattering the brush bow. He was glad Claire had an experienced crew in the Sommers.

See you in Nome. Mushers said that in lieu of wishing each other luck. But Claire's kiss had promised more than just luck. It felt nice to be wanted. Damn nice.

Do you have family worrying about you?

He hadn't talked to his parents since the night his dad threw him out. He didn't blame them. He accepted the consequences of his actions, cut himself off from anybody who knew the asshole he'd been. Dad was almost seventy now, Mom two years younger. Did they worry about him? Miss him?

Ah, hell.

"John, start putting booties on the dogs," Dillon said. "Leave Clyde for last. He'll rip 'em off as fast as you put 'em on."

"Got it."

As the sun pushed high above the mountains, driving the temperature to twenty-five degrees, Claire heard the drumbeats and chants of an Alaska Native dance group near the starting line at Fourth and D. People wrapped their hands around cups of hot soda from street-side vendors while a trio of women sang the national anthem. The Iditarod Board of Directors president, the mayor of Anchorage, and the governor of Alaska took turns thanking spectators and wishing the mushers a great race. The nonstop yips and whines of the dogs grew, drowning out the last speaker, as the teams began lining up. At 10:00 a.m., a race official counted down: "Five, four, three, two, one!" And the first team, driven by someone who had been named an honorary musher for their contributions to dog sledding, headed out of Anchorage, beginning the race. Starting at 10:02, the competitors followed at two-minute intervals. People cheered and clapped from the sidelines as each team made its way down Fourth.

At 10:34 a.m., Claire heard the countdown for bib eighteen over the loudspeaker and knew Dillon was on his way. In less than ten minutes, it would be her turn. From the back of her sled, she regarded her team, now in harness, being guided to the starting queue by Iditarod Trail Committee volunteers. Handsome, his head up and tail whipping, shared the lead with Ranger. Toolik, a tan-and-white giveaway from Shaktoolik, ran swing next to Treker, a smart little female with a peppy attitude. Trouble, a brown-and-black mutt with a notched left ear for a fight trophy, teamed with Pepper, whose mild temper Claire hoped would keep the scrapper pacified.

Next came the sunshine boys, Singer and Riley. Singer tipped his head back in a boisterous song while Riley grinned at his Iditarod volunteer. Zach, named after a friend of Matt's who had died on Denali, lunged in his harness and danced on his hind legs, eager to get down the trail. He was fast, with a die-hard drive. Claire paired the compact husky with Ginny, a quiet, long-legged female who preferred to remain invisible but was a dependable follower. And in wheel position were the even-tempered sisters, Sugar and Daisy.

A crew of veterinarians had examined the dogs, and the race marshal inspected her sled for required gear, which included a symbolic letter to be delivered in Nome as tribute to the carriers who used to deliver mail by dog teams.

Her IditaRider, Dr. Lee Osgood from Texas, was bundled in the sled, ready for his eleven-mile thrill. Once again, Claire prayed she didn't give him more of a thrill than he had paid for. In tow a few feet behind her, Matt drove the tag sled. Janey and Andy were in charge of getting the dog truck with the rest of her team and gear to Campbell Airstrip, the second checkpoint. Then they would reload everything and drive to Willow, the third checkpoint, for tomorrow's official restart. The open waters of the glacier-fed Knik River were often impassable for sled dogs, and the Department of Transportation deemed it unsafe for mushers to use the highway bridges, making it necessary to shuttle teams between checkpoints two and three. Anchorage was just for show and did not count toward a team's official race time.

From Willow, she and her dogs would be on their own. By tomorrow evening, they'd reach Yentna Station, the next checkpoint, forty-two miles from Willow. Then it was another thirty miles to Skwentna and their first food drop.

One checkpoint at a time, Matt emphasized whenever she got herself worked up over keeping all the details straight— where the worst sections were, what to look for, when to stop. *Just take it one checkpoint at a time.*

And then Claire heard her name over the loudspeaker. Volunteers held her eager team at the start banner. Her sled secured and her heart pounding in excitement, she took a few quick seconds to trot the length of the gangline and give each dog a reassuring pat or hug. She felt the eager tension in their tight muscles, saw the anticipation in their eyes. Singer tipped his head back and howled another tune, making Claire laugh. She pulled Trouble's neck line out of his mouth and said, "Knock it off. You're not leaving without us." Handsome and Ranger bounced and pulled against their tug lines impatiently. "Soon, guys, real soon." Ginny tucked her tail and laid her ears back, doing her best to look inconspicuous. "It's all right, girl. You can do this." Someone thrust a microphone at Claire. She smiled and waved. "Hi, Dad!"

"Fifteen seconds!"

Claire dashed back to the sled. Matt gave her a thumbs-up and she returned the gesture.

"Five! Four! Three! Two!"

Claire nodded at the volunteers to release her team. "One! GO!"

Chapter 11

Thousands of people waved and cheered from the sidelines as Claire's dogs lunged down Fourth Avenue. They plowed through the churned tracks of previous teams, trampling dog poop and thrown booties. Cameras flashed. Dr. Osgood laughed and Claire joined him with a whoop.

Ginny shied from the noisy attention and sidled into Zach, breaking his rhythm. "That's a good girl, Gin. Straight on." The leggy female responded to the encouragement and pulled into her harness.

"They look great!" Dr. Osgood shouted.

"Yes, they do! Thank you!"

The soft snow gave the dogs a workout and kept their

speed down as they approached Cordova Street, where a sharp right turn would be Claire's first test at keeping her rider in the sled. She'd heard stories about teams taking it too fast, rolling the sled and dumping rider and musher in front of onlookers, or a tag sled slamming into the berm of snow piled at the corner.

"We're going slow enough that it shouldn't be a problem," she said, as much to reassure herself as to put her rider at ease.

Handsome anticipated the turn and started to cut into it too soon. "Stay haw, Handsome! Stay haw!" The team straightened, swung wide, and took the corner like pros. "Good dogs!" She glanced back and saw Matt still behind her and upright on the tag sled.

"Woohoo!" he shouted, punching the air with a gloved fist.

Claire laughed and faced forward. "We're on our way now!"

Dr. Osgood slapped his mittened hands together. If his continuous bursts of laughter were any indication, the man was having the time of his life.

Twelve blocks later, the trail dropped down a hill to Mulcahy Stadium and joined the Anchorage bike- and ski-path system, a greenbelt that ran along Chester Creek through stands of tall, straight birch and occasional culverts under roadways.

Ginny shied into Zach at the first culvert. "It's okay, Gin. Good girl." Claire could understand the dog's skittishness. The noise and enclosed space were a stark contrast to the remote wilderness trails they'd trained on. She had questioned Matt's advice to put the quiet, easy-to-spook female on the team out of Anchorage over one of the calmer dogs, like Groucho.

"It'll be a good way for her to get acclimated," he said. "She'll come around."

By the third culvert, his prediction proved correct. Ginny kept pace with her teammates, giving the underpasses no more than a brief glance.

They crossed a pedestrian bridge, and a sharp left took them by the university and behind a residential area where well-wishers handed wrapped, fresh-baked muffins to the mushers and IditaRiders as they passed. Claire tucked hers into her handlebar bag for later.

The trail followed the south shore of University Lake, crossed another pedestrian overpass, then dropped onto Tudor Road for part of a mile. The crowds had thinned, and Claire saw her dogs settle into a comfortable rhythm, tails relaxed, ears flopping. They felt more in their element now. Two sharp turns took them onto the Tozier Track system of tree-lined dog trails through Centennial Park, a huge undeveloped area. Claire felt some of the tension in her own shoulders ease at the more familiar terrain.

A short while later, her team followed one final culvert onto Campbell Airstrip, where Janey and Andy waited with the truck, marking the end of the first stage of the race.

The restart of the Iditarod the following afternoon repeated Saturday's ceremonial start in Anchorage, minus the city streets and tall buildings. Mushers spent the morning cooking dog chow to haul in coolers for stops along the trail. On the lake at Willow, spectators lined the starting chute and beyond. The temperature sat at eighteen degrees under a retina-piercing blue sky. Smoke spiraled from family grills, filling the air with the smells of burger patties and barbecue sauce and giving the event a picnic atmosphere.

Mushers and handlers unloaded their entire teams this time, fed them, and got them into booties and harnesses. Some of the dogs sported colorful coats in anticipation of a cool evening. Now that the IditaRiders were gone, mushers packed their sleds with all the gear needed to survive the Alaskan bush, along with GPS trackers that would transmit data for each team—including speed, location, run-and-rest cycles, and air temperature—to Iditarod officials. This was information the mushers themselves couldn't see.

Yesterday had been for show. Today, mushers wore their game faces, and the dogs were noisier and more animated, ready to get down to business. At 2:00 p.m., teams would begin leaving the checkpoint.

Dillon looked forward to the simplicity of life on the trail—no phones, no demands or interruptions, just the uncomplicated task of tending to the dogs. With his sled packed and his team ready, he went to look for Claire.

He found her in the classic stooped-over musher's position, putting fluorescent-orange booties on one of her dogs. "Hey," he said.

She looked up and smiled. "Hey yourself."

"How'd it go yesterday?"

"Great. Only a thousand more miles to go." She gave her dog a pat on the shoulder and straightened. "And you?"

"Brian took a dive off the tag sled on Cordova."

"I heard about that. Is he all right?"

"Yeah. He's with the dog truck, being consoled by a cute young lady who goes to his high school."

Claire put her hand over her heart and sighed. "I'm crushed."

Dillon grunted. "I'm sure you are. So," he said as he moved closer and she did the same, "does this mean you're available once we get to Nome?"

"What did you have in mind?"

"Dinner and dancing at the Bering West."

"You have dancing?"

He pretended to take offense at her surprise. "Of course." She'd find out soon enough that the music came from a jukebox and the dance floor was the size of a tabletop. A very small tabletop.

"What's on the menu?"

She may have been asking about the dinner special, but the look she gave him said otherwise. He stood only half a step away from her, close enough to keep his answer between them. "Whatever you want." He couldn't help himself. None of the reasons he'd recited in his head for not getting tangled up with the lady lawyer mattered a damn when she fixed him with those dark whiskey eyes.

Her smile stopped his breath. "I'll be waiting."

Chapter 12

Tailgate partyers along the trail heading out of Willow shouted encouragement to the mushers, but their enthusiasm distracted some of the dogs. Ginny shied when a snow machine buzzed too close, while Mama's Boy and Groucho attempted to track each delectable food odor. "No junk food for you guys," Claire told them. "On by."

She'd seen this part of the trail before—an easy stretch of flatland to low rolling hills along the frozen Susitna River—on one of her qualifying races. The dogs, still jazzed from the excitement of the restart, set a fast pace. Claire rode the drag occasionally to keep them from burning out, but she had to admit the speed felt invigorating.

Two and a half hours after the restart, she stopped trail-side to snack her athletes, the first of many stops she'd make at two-to-three-hour intervals throughout the race. Keeping the dogs hydrated and loaded with calories—a minimum of eleven thousand a day per dog—was critical. Other teams glided past as she doled out frozen fish and high-density kibble. She grabbed an energy bar for herself and washed it down with a fruit drink.

The last of the day's sun faded the sky to stonewashed violet as she and her team arrived at the Yentna Station checkpoint, located at the confluence of the Susitna and Yentna Rivers. Iditarod volunteers helped her remove her bib and recorded her check-in time. The log showed Dillon had blown through the checkpoint fifteen minutes ahead of her. The two-story Yentna Station Roadhouse tempted her with a warm fire and a hot meal free to Iditarod mushers, but staying at the crowded checkpoint wasn't in her race plan. She and her dogs pushed on.

Bonfires along the banks of the Yentna River laced the evening air with woodsmoke and the smells of wiener roasts and charred marshmallows. Fans settled in for an all-night vigil of race watching and partying. Claire pulled her team over to let another team pass, and a short woman bundled in fur handed her a hot dog still warm from the fire.

"You need to keep up your strength," the woman said, flashing a broad smile.

"Thank you. It looks delicious." And it was. Mustard, ketchup, onions—the best hot dog she'd ever eaten.

As she drove into her first night on the Iditarod, the temperature dropped to ten below. The cold burned her mouth and nose, and she pulled her neck gaiter up higher. Toasty in her insulated gear, she absorbed her surroundings, took in the fact that she was actually here, on the Iditarod Trail. Stars too numerous to count pulsed in the clear sky. She turned her headlamp on but then turned it off again because it spoiled the view. The dogs didn't need the light.

She stopped trailside prior to reaching Skwentna to feed her dogs the meal she and the Sommers had cooked that morning. The food had to be kept in the cooler so it wouldn't freeze. Once the dogs had eaten and curled up for a snooze, Claire managed to catch a nap on top of her sled bag before the sounds of another team passing in the dark woke her.

They reached Skwentna at 3:30 a.m. Claire followed the volunteers waving glow sticks to collect the first of her food-drop bags, then blew through the checkpoint. Her dogs needed little coaxing.

An hour after dawn on day two, they made the Finger Lake checkpoint, which was bordered by a line of timber at the base of the Alaska Range. A checker wearing a bright-yellow vest over his parka welcomed her. "Bib number?"

"Twenty-two."

He recorded the information on his clipboard and looked at his watch. "Time is eight thirty-seven. How many dogs?"

"Sixteen." Claire signed the check-in log.

"Are you staying?"

"Yes."

"Okay, there are half bales and full bales, HEET, and water on your right."

"Great. Thanks." Claire pulled up the hook. "Hup. Good dogs."

Once she'd loaded the supplies on her sled, a volunteer showed her where to park her team. They'd been on the trail for eighteen hours and had covered 112 miles. Claire planned to wait out the heat of the day in Finger Lake and give her dogs a good rest before tackling the Happy River Steps and the side hills of Happy River Canyon. The next hundred miles or so would be some of their toughest.

The dogs wasted no time settling in. Ginny curled into a tight, unobtrusive ball. Singer and Riley rolled in the snow and pawed the air. Riley was minus a bootie. Again. Trouble nipped at Pepper for encroaching on his space, and Groucho barked like a skipping record, impatient to eat. Claire tossed a scoop of kibble onto the snow in front of each dog and followed it up with slices of frozen lamb.

She began spreading straw for their bedding, and a volunteer veterinarian came by to do a HAWL (heart, hydration, appetite and attitude, weight, and lungs) examination on each dog. Claire showed the vet her yellow book documenting previous mandatory checks.

"How'd they look on the trail?" the vet asked as she manipulated Handsome's right front leg, looking for sprains or soreness. "Any concerns?"

"They did great," Claire said. "The trail's been perfect. Nice base under the snow."

While the woman continued her exam on the rest of the team, Claire finished laying out straw and started removing booties. She ran her fingers between pads to clear any ice accumulation, checked for abrasions, and applied zinc oxide ointment to keep their paws soft and dry. Riley's rear left paw showed a little redness but no breaks in the skin. Claire rubbed an anti-inflammatory on it to be safe.

With Groucho, Sam, Mama's Boy, and Harmony rounding out Saturday's ceremonial lineup, she had sixty-four paws to inspect. Zach got tired of waiting and chewed one of his booties off. "Darn it," Claire scolded, poking her finger through the soggy hole he'd made. His ears flattened against his head. "Don't give me that sad look. Luckily for you and Riley, I packed extras."

The veterinarian confirmed what Claire already knew: her athletes were in good health. She could pull up the hook and get back on the trail right now and they'd be fine with it. But she didn't want to push them or herself.

She set up the alcohol cooker, dumped in HEET, lit it, and set a pot of water to boil. The Alaska Range watched and waited. Claire paused to lean back and study its intimidating snowy peaks and icy ravines. Later that afternoon, she and her dogs would take on the challenge of reaching the other side. *My God.*

Dillon was up there somewhere. He may have even checked out of Rainy Pass by now. She hadn't seen him since the restart in Willow yesterday afternoon. According to the log, he had stayed in Skwentna for a few hours but had already checked out when she got there. He had gone through Finger Lake two and a half hours before she and her team arrived.

Suggesting she might finish the race ahead of him had been an entertaining thought while it lasted. She smiled to herself. As long as she got her team to Nome, making him wait for her had its appeal too.

Chapter 13

After a five-hour rest at the Rainy Pass checkpoint, elevation 1,800 feet, Dillon and his team began the long uphill climb toward the summit of Rainy Pass, which cut through the mountains at 3,160 feet—the highest point on the Iditarod Trail. A layer of clouds rolled over the surrounding peaks, and the air cooled as the afternoon grew late. Dillon couldn't have asked for a nicer day. When he came through this area two years ago, whiteout conditions had obliterated the trail and reduced visibility, making for an ass-tightening adventure. But even on a bad day, this country fed his soul. He breathed deep, pulling it into his lungs.

"Looking good up there, Chevy." He'd put Chevron in lead

with Bonnie, giving Maverick a rest in the middle of the pack. They'd need the little dog's agility over Mav's speed once they started their descent into the gorge. "That's my girl, Bonnie."

The trail steepened as they neared the summit. Dillon pedaled from the back of the sled to help his dogs push through the soft snow of avalanche territory. "Come on, kids. Hike." They traveled face-first into the wind channeling down the valley. The muscles in Dillon's legs burned. "Almost there. Hike. Hike." The mind-numbing physical exertion made it easy to shut off the claustrophobia threatening to awaken from years of hibernation. He pushed himself hard, taking as much of the sled's weight off his dogs as possible.

And then they were over the top and dropping into the heart of the Alaska Range. The trail narrowed and twisted through stunted willow brush and rocky ravines, descending 1,000 feet in five and a half miles. Yesterday's serpentine steps into Happy River Canyon had been a piece of cake in comparison. Dillon wondered if Claire had made it down the steps yet, then shoved the thought aside as the sled slammed over a snag. *Keep your mind in the game.*

The team approached a boulder jutting into the trail. "Easy. Take it easy." Dillon rode the drag to check their speed, but that made the sled more difficult to steer. Once the dogs had cleared the boulder, he let up on the drag and the sled slipped nicely around the obstruction.

There was no time to pat himself on the back. "Come on. Easy," he told the dogs as they approached the next obstacle in the trail. Though spent from his push to the summit, Dillon couldn't afford to relax. He alternately rode the drag and maneuvered to avoid the pits and bumps and snags of Pass Fork until the trail opened onto the wooded valley of Dalzell Creek. "All right. Good job, kids."

The smooth run lasted a couple miles before the trail swung to the south side of the valley and made a sharp climb to a forested shelf. Dillon braced for the roller-coaster drop into Dalzell Gorge.

"Hang on. Slow. Take it slow."

For the next two miles, the trail descended 200 feet, jumping back and forth across Dalzell Creek on narrow snow-and-ice bridges spanning open water. Trail marker ribbons tied to the trees snapped by. Mountain cliffs closed in on both sides, mocking Dillon's claustrophobia.

Guy's hind legs flew out from under him, but the team's momentum helped him regain his footing in a couple quick strides. "Watch yourself, big man. That's my powerhouse."

Thanks to recent snowfall and the great work of the Iditarod trail-breaking crew, the going was easier than Dillon had seen it in the past. He was thinking they might actually get through the gorge without any problems when the middle of the team cut a turn too tight, tangling Guy and Annie in a clump of willow. "Whoa! Wait!" Setting the hook, he tramped to the front of the sled to free his wheel dogs and line out the team. Trudging back to the sled, he pulled up the hook. "Okay, take it easy."

A few yards later the team tangled again, and he repeated the process. The two-mile stretch of trail felt like twenty before it leveled and broke out onto the Tatina River.

"Good job, kids. We did it. Straight ahead."

Glare ice caught the last of the day's light, making the surface of the frozen river shine like wet glass. The dogs kept a steady pace. Dillon spotted overflow—where water below pushed up and over the ice—along the bank, far enough away that it wasn't a threat.

At 7:15 p.m., they reached the Rohn checkpoint—a BLM

(Bureau of Land Management) cabin sheltered from the wind by tall spruce trees. Ideal for getting some rest. Other teams had arrived ahead of them and were in various stages of settling in.

"I'm staying," Dillon told the checker.

In the time it took to collect his drop bags, lay out straw for his dogs, inspect paws, dispense snacks, set up the cooker, and shovel snow to melt for water, exhaustion set in hard. He'd slept maybe six hours in two days and 188 miles. Numb, he sat with his headlamp aimed inside the three-gallon pot and stared at the tiny bubbles forming and bursting on the bottom. *What's that saying about a watched pot?*

His eyelids drooped.

A dog's sharp yip yanked him awake. Bands of green and blue shimmered across the night sky.

I never get tired of seeing that.

Claire's words brought her to the forefront of his thoughts again. Her eyes made him think of Jack Daniel's, the seduction of that first swallow and the warmth it generated in his belly. He hadn't taken a drink in six years, nine months, and… long enough he'd lost track. But the sharp, not-quite-sweet taste lingered like the aftertaste of Claire's mouth pressed to his.

Thinking of her made him yearn for tangled sheets, skin pressed to skin, things he hadn't allowed himself to need in a long time. Wanting her was complicated, linked to a past he'd worked hard to bury. He'd told her she could have whatever she wanted, but was he prepared to give it?

What if she wanted the truth?

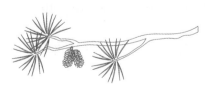

Claire and her team made good time down the Happy River Steps—a narrow, tree-lined wild ride of switchbacks that descended the canyon. She was confident the guy with the video camera at the bottom of the last step had shot prime footage of her demonstration on how to navigate a heavy sled while being dragged behind it. She wished she'd given him her contact information so he could send her a copy.

Her dogs rested at the Rainy Pass checkpoint and she dried clothes. The heat inside the lodge clogged her sinuses, and the concentration of smells was a harsh contrast to the cold, almost odorless outside air. Five hours later, they pushed on under the full moon's ivory light, traveling through miles of ethereal shadows. Dillon hadn't exaggerated when he said the Iditarod Trail had a raw beauty. Even the sharp, cold wind moaned a song uniquely its own as Claire and her dogs crossed over the summit of Rainy Pass.

She spilled the sled twice on the stretch down Pass Fork, and the adrenaline-pumping drop into Dalzell Gorge tested her sled-driving skills as she skirted rocks that didn't get out of the way. They reached the Rohn checkpoint at 3:25 on Tuesday morning, missing Dillon by four hours.

On the seventy-five-mile stretch to Nikolai, beleaguering winds swept the sandbars and gravel of the South Fork Kuskokwim River clear of snow. Claire muscled the sled around driftwood tangles and glare ice. She and her team confronted the Buffalo Tunnels—narrow tracts of exposed dirt, rock, and tussocks wallowed out by roaming buffalo— and managed to avoid any wrong turns. She stopped trailside to snack the dogs, check their feet, and repair the sled's cracked brush bow with duct tape and wire.

Crossing the Farewell Burn—once a wicked path of snags and stumps through the remains of a massive forest fire that consumed over a million acres in the late '70s, and now a groomed stretch of intermittent dirt and new growth—she stopped again to snack, check feet, and replace sled runners. She met one challenge after another with increased confidence in herself and her team. Muscles she didn't know she had complained from pumping and ski poling to help her dogs power up hillsides and through soft snow. Fogged by lack of sleep, she found that everything took longer than expected, from dog care to reaching the next checkpoint.

She'd never felt so alive.

Behind them, the Alaska Range stretched northeast, now more respected friend than imposing foe. Low clouds concealed the highest of its stunning, rugged peaks. Claire dug out her camera, remembered telling Dillon about the man it used to belong to, and smiled. *Yep. One hell of a vacation.* She took several pictures before moving on.

The trail over the windblown flats heading into Nikolai ran west-northwest, a level straightaway of punchy snow and sparse brush that seemed to go on forever. Claire talked to her athletes often. "Good dogs!" "How's my Handsome doing up there?" "Straight on, Ranger." "Looking good, Ginny girl." The constant chatter kept them alert and prevented her from nodding off.

When she checked into the quaint Athabascan village of Nikolai at 5:28 p.m., they'd been on the trail almost nine hours and were 263 miles from Anchorage.

Chapter 14

The onset of evening cast long dark fingers across the landscape as Dillon and his team reached Big River, the halfway point between Nikolai and McGrath. The trail took an abrupt drop and turned west, heading toward the Kuskokwim River. For the past three hours, they'd been cutting cross-country along a series of frozen lakes and swamps interspersed with wooded stretches in a blur of sameness. Travel on the river was hard and fast, and the temperature was dropping. Dillon decided to give his dogs a few more miles to shed the day's heat before stopping to put coats on them. He couldn't have been more pleased with their performance so far: healthy appetites, good skin elasticity, positive attitudes.

Their five-hour stay in Nikolai had done them good, and the mound of spaghetti the locals served him at the school cafeteria had been worthy of seconds. It sure beat reconstituted stroganoff with mystery meat from a foil packet. He wondered how far back Claire was and hoped she wouldn't miss out on the feast.

The trail climbed the bank and headed into the woods again. "Easy," he said. "Let's not get wrapped around a tree."

Half a second before Bonnie and Maverick ran out of sight around a bend, he saw their ears shoot forward and felt a burst of speed from the team. "Easy. What is it?"

The sled cleared the corner, and he saw a thousand-pound bull moose in the middle of the trail, head down and swinging its massive rack side to side, ready to charge.

Dillon stood on the brake and yelled, "Whoa!" But the team's momentum tangled Bonnie and Maverick under the moose's belly before churning to a stop. Dillon stomped the hook as Maverick bit at the moose's hind leg. It kicked out and Bonnie caught the blow broadside. Her high yelp cut the air, and she went down. Chevron and Rocky snarled and lunged against the snow hook to defend their leaders. The moose reared and raked at them with its front legs. The dogs dodged its deadly hooves. Dillon bellowed, "No! God damn it, get out of here!" The dogs growled and barked and whined. The moose lowered its head and rumbled deep in its throat. The air reeked of dank fur and rage. Dillon threw his gloves aside and dug the .45 out of the handlebar bag. Heart-tearing screams rent the air: his own and his dogs'. The throb of his pulse drowned them out. Time slowed.

He aimed and fired.

The pistol bucked, no louder than a cap gun. The smell of cordite mixed with the stench of stale pizza. The bullet made impact. The suspect took a step back, then recoiled and dropped to his knees, grabbing at the glistening wet spot spreading across his chest. Surprised eyes, too young, pleaded for help. Bloody fingers reached out...

A dog cried. Dillon blinked. He saw the moose lumber down the trail and into the woods. The snow at the front of his team bled.

Chapter 15

Claire reached McGrath a few minutes before nine on the morning of day four. Her dogs looked good enough to keep going a couple more hours, and that's what she planned to do once she picked up her bags and swapped her broken sled for the one she'd dropped at the checkpoint. Though McGrath was a popular spot for mushers to take their mandatory twenty-four-hour layover, Matt had suggested she avoid the hectic hub and take her twenty-four at the next checkpoint, Takotna, eighteen miles away.

But when she signed the log, she noticed Dillon had checked in nine hours earlier. "Bib eighteen's still here?" she asked the volunteer.

"He tangled with a moose and needed time to get his dogs taken care of."

"Anything serious?"

"One of his leaders had to be dropped."

Claire's stomach clenched. "I changed my mind. I'm staying."

At the McGrath checkpoint, the water cooler outside the laundromat made dog food prep easier and quicker. Since she was staying, Claire intended to take advantage of the coin-operated shower too. And to get sleep. Hours of it, if possible. Her boots felt like they were weighed down by thick mud as she went through the motions of feeding, checking feet, laying out straw, and putting coats on her marathon runners to keep them comfortable during their much-deserved snooze.

Before she could get any sleep herself, though, she wanted to find Dillon and see how he was doing. She passed by his dogs curled in slumber. Bonnie wasn't among them. His other lead dog—*Maverick?*—wore a heat wrap on one of his front legs. An injured or sick dog was Claire's greatest fear. She could only imagine what Dillon must have been going through.

Since he wasn't with his dogs, Claire decided to try the community center. The smells of fried potatoes, bacon, sausage, and fresh-brewed coffee distracted her as she went inside. A clatter of kitchen noise competed with scattered conversations, punctuated by the occasional belch or gaping yawn or burst of laughter from mushers in varying stages of exhaustion and hunger. Cold-weather gear hung from slumped shoulders and littered the backs of chairs in a riot of colors. The concentration of body odors pressured Claire's sinuses.

She spotted Dillon sitting at a table in the corner, his hands anchored around a mug. When she pulled out the empty chair next to him, he started and glanced up. The haunted look in his eyes scared her.

"Hey," she said as she sat down.

"Hey yourself," he answered, his voice raw.

"Is Bonnie okay?"

"She has a concussion. Needs stitches. Nothing she won't recover from, thank God."

"That's a relief. How are you doing?"

He stared at the mug in his hands. "I can't stop shaking."

"I'm sorry, Dillon." She ached to hold him, to tell him he'd be all right when she really didn't know if he would. She didn't want to presume she knew what he felt. And she sure as hell didn't want to cry, but tears pressed behind her eyes. She fell back on the one thing people always relied on in moments of hardship or crisis. "Have you eaten yet?"

He frowned as though he couldn't remember, then shook his head. "No."

"How about I buy you breakfast?"

"Sure. Thanks."

She'd been joking about buying. McGrath's volunteer-staffed kitchen rivaled any five-star restaurant, and the food was free to mushers. Claire did her best not to drool as she balanced two paper plates piled with pancakes, sausage links, bacon, and scrambled eggs to the table. After setting the plates down, she snagged a bacon strip with one hand

and extracted the cold mug from Dillon's grasp with the other. "Refill?"

"Please."

When she returned, the half-eaten bacon dangling from her mouth and a brimming mug of black coffee in each hand, she caught Dillon attempting to cut into his pancakes. His hand shook so badly Claire feared he'd break his plastic fork, but she stopped short of grabbing it from him to help. It didn't take a mind reader to know he'd object to having his food cut up for him like a child.

And he was pissed. She saw it in the tightness around his mouth and eyes.

She sat and dug into her food. "Wanna talk about it?" she asked around a mouthful of eggs loaded with cheese and ham. Divine.

"No." He gave up on the fork, grabbed a pancake from the top of the stack, rolled a sausage link in it, and shoved it into his mouth.

Claire slathered butter and syrup on her own pancakes and consumed them so fast she barely tasted them. "It feels like I haven't eaten in months," she groaned.

Dillon mumbled something that sounded like agreement and wrapped another sausage in a pancake. "I'll trade you my bacon for your sausage," he said before stuffing his face.

Claire made the trade. She preferred bacon anyway. By the fourth pancake-wrapped link, she noticed his trembling had eased. He attempted the fork again to eat his eggs, this time with more success. Satisfied that his nerves had calmed and he seemed to be doing better, Claire went back to the kitchen for an enormous gooey cinnamon roll and more coffee.

"Get your own," she said when she saw him eyeing her plate.

The corner of his mouth lifted. "Spoilsport."

She watched him walk away, saw the fatigue pulling at his body, and wished he'd talk to her. But in her present state, she probably wouldn't remember anything he said anyway. Lack of sleep fuzzed her brain and slowed her movements as she buttered her cinnamon roll and took a huge bite. Then another. And another.

"Claire?"

Her head snapped up. She realized she'd been about to nod off into what was left of her cinnamon roll.

Dillon slanted her a smile. "You've got butter on your nose."

"Oh." She swiped at her face with her napkin and noticed the almost finished hunk of chocolate cake in front of him. "How long have I been sitting here comatose?"

"Not long."

"Liar. Guess I'd better find someplace to sleep."

"There's space in the back," he said, pointing. "Follow the snoring."

Claire tried to laugh, but it took too much energy just to stand. All the coffee and sugary treats in the state of Alaska couldn't keep her awake right now. "Are you staying your twenty-four here?"

"Yes."

"Then I'll catch up with you later."

He nodded. "Thanks for breakfast."

Three other mushers were already zonked out in the sleeping area. Claire found a space on the thick carpet as far away as possible from the unidentifiable lump snoring in the corner and spread out her sleeping bag. She set her alarm to go off in four hours and tucked it against her belly so it wouldn't disturb anybody else when it did. Using her parka for a pillow, she pulled the sleeping bag over her head and gave in to exhaustion.

Bloody fingers reached for him, clawed at his face. He tried to fight off the ghost-white figure drained of life, but his leaden arms refused to move. Desperate to escape, he ran. His heavy boots slid on empty pizza boxes. Room after room, a maze of emptiness and hallways went on until his legs trembled. He couldn't find the way out. Door after door led him deeper in. His heart hammered. He struggled for air. *Breathe.* He tried to yell but could only force a choked, guttural sound past his raw throat. The toe of his boot jammed into a soft lump on the floor and he fell hard to his knees, biting his tongue. He crawled over the lump, his hands sinking into fur. A dog. A white dog covered in blood.

No! God, no!

Dillon jolted. Claire leaned over him, her hair tangled. *What's she doing here? She needs to get out...*

"Are you awake?" she asked.

Not trapped. Not crawling in blood. "Where am I?"

"In the mushers' sleeping area. Sounded like you were having a nightmare."

Yes. His gut tightened. A nightmare. One he hadn't had in years. Only it was different this time, more intense. Bonnie was hurt. "Shit." He sat up and rubbed at his face. An iron taste in his mouth told him he hadn't imagined biting his tongue. "Did I say anything?"

A woman lying a few feet away mumbled, "Loud enough to wake the dead."

Someone else grunted confirmation.

Embarrassed, Dillon muttered, "Sorry. I'm leaving."

Claire's alarm clock went off and she cringed. "Looks like I am too. See you for dinner?"

Dillon raked his fingers through his hair. He realized he didn't want to be alone with his thoughts. "I'll buy this time."

She gave a tired smile. "And I'll try not to fall asleep in my dessert."

Chapter 16

Located on the Kuskokwim River, the village of McGrath (population around 400) functioned as a communication, transportation, and supply center for interior Alaska. The village was roughly equidistant from Anchorage to the south and Fairbanks to the north, and although no roads connected it to either, river access and a full-service airport—along with restaurants and lodges—made it a popular destination. An almost constant drone of air traffic and snow machines assaulted the senses, yet Handsome's head lifted at Claire's approach.

"Did you have a nice nap?" she asked, giving his ears a rub. He closed his eyes and soaked up the attention. Ranger yawned and whined for his turn. Claire went down the line, greeting each one and administering rubdowns. Their unplanned stop in McGrath turned out to be advantageous. The midday temperature had climbed to twenty-five degrees, too warm for the dogs to cover long distances without frequent water breaks. Tomorrow's forecast promised colder conditions.

"How about a tasty frozen lamb strip to snack on while I cook up some chow?" Singer tossed his head back and howled. Groucho, who had been doing his best to ignore her, sat up and licked his chops.

Once Claire had her dogs checked, fed, and comfortable, she dug out her personal bag and headed for the shower. She lathered her hair twice while the hot water loosened tight muscles and made her feel human again.

When she entered the community center a short while later, the smells of steak and potatoes made her stomach rumble. She didn't see Dillon as she put in her request with the kitchen staff. The table they'd shared earlier was vacant. She poured herself a cup of coffee and grabbed a seat to wait. It gave her an opportunity to people watch, pick up bits of conversation, and note the diversity of mushers—what they wore and what they joked about. Some discussed trail conditions and strategy and how their dogs were performing. They were indomitable spirits reenacting the decades-old tradition of honoring the first diphtheria serum run to Nome. And she was a part of it.

Out here in the middle of nowhere, her dad would say. She wished she could share the experience with him but knew he wouldn't understand. Mama would have. She'd probably have insisted on racing her own team. The thought made Claire smile into her coffee mug.

Movement at the entrance caught her attention. It was Dillon. He'd cleaned up. And shaved? She waved to get his attention, drawing a nod and smile from him. Her pulse tripped over itself. *Darn it, he has a nice smile. And a nice way of walking, even exhausted as he must still be.* She could get used to watching him enter a room.

"Ooh, look at the pretty boy," a burly musher with a tangled mustache and a broad grin commented from the other end of the table.

"Must have a date," someone else cooed.

Dillon slanted them a wry grin of his own. "Jealous?"

"You bet!"

They shared a good-natured laugh. Claire stood when Dillon got close enough to touch. She ran a hand over his smooth cheek. "Is this for me?"

"It sure wasn't for those jokers."

Warmth flushed through her at the glint in his eyes. She drew his face closer and kissed him, eliciting cheers and a wolf whistle from their audience.

"Excuse me, honey." Claire looked over at the dark-haired kitchen volunteer setting a plate of food on the table. "Your dinner's ready." The woman winked. "I can keep it warm for you if you'd like to…you know." She tossed Dillon a quick glance, then looked back at Claire with a sly smile.

Her implication sent Claire's warm flush rocketing to her cheeks. "I uh…" she stammered. "No, thank you. I'll eat now."

The woman sighed her disappointment. "Whatever you want."

Whatever you want. Dillon had said those words to her four days ago. She turned and found him watching her. She wanted *him.* Pure and simple. Awareness flared in his eyes, and she thought she finally understood the concept of swooning. If not for the support of the table against her leg, she wouldn't have been surprised to find herself dropping to the floor in a faint. It had to be exhaustion and hunger. *You don't do soft and vulnerable, remember?*

Her stomach chose that moment to rumble again.

Dillon smiled. "You'd better feed that thing."

Claire tucked her hair behind her ear and gave a self-conscious laugh.

Dillon enjoyed hearing Claire laugh. He enjoyed watching her eat, the automatic way she hooked her hair behind her ear while shoveling mashed potatoes into her mouth. He hadn't realized how much he missed her until she showed up at the checkpoint. He enjoyed her company. Being with her made it easy to attribute the flashes of darkness to sleep deprivation and concern over his injured dogs. *That's all it is,* he told himself.

But maybe I could have acted quicker—

"You really packed a razor?" Claire asked, slowing her potato shoveling to cut a bite of steak.

He'd opted for biscuits with sausage gravy and green beans. "I bought a cheap disposable at a store down the street."

"I should check it out later. I'd kill for a bag of barbecue potato chips right now."

"You're kidding." He forked a hunk of biscuit into his mouth.

"Oh, please. Don't you have a guilty pleasure? Something you'd eat in spite of the heartburn?"

"Pepperoni sticks," he mumbled around his chewing.

"Excuse me?"

"You know, the kind they keep in a plastic container by the checkout."

"Gross."

"You're the one who asked." A forkful of beans hovered over his plate. "When we get to Nome, I'll buy you the biggest bag of barbecue chips I can find."

"*Potato* chips, not corn."

"Got it."

"And I'll buy you a container of pepperoni." She gave a dramatic shudder and muttered, "Along with a tin of breath mints."

He laughed.

"Seriously, I'm not kissing pepperoni breath."

Dillon liked the idea of more kissing. He raised his coffee mug in a toast. "You've got a deal."

She tapped her mug rim against his. "You heading out tonight?"

"Midnight."

"Think you'll get a little more sleep before you leave?"

"No." Then, because his answer sounded abrupt, he justified it: "I won't have time." It was closer to the truth than not. Before leaving, he needed to feed his dogs and get a vet to check Maverick's leg once more to make sure he was up to running. The fierce little husky had ridden into McGrath in the sled bag with Bonnie because of a limp, but the vet had suggested a heat wrap and rest might be enough to keep him in the race. Dillon hoped so. He hated dropping dogs. Losing both of his best leaders would break his heart.

"Are you going to be okay?" Claire asked. "I mean, the moose attack hit you pretty hard. Dropping Bonnie—"

His guard went up at her concern. He couldn't help it. After years of practice, he had no control over the automatic reaction. "I'll be okay." If he repeated it often enough, he might even start believing it.

He saw the disappointment in her eyes. Then she looked away, as though too tired to care. That stung, but he knew he deserved it. "Good," she said. She pushed away from the table and began collecting her trash. "Thanks for dinner. And the kiss. I'm going to get some sleep."

Dillon put his hand on her arm so she'd look at him. "Thank you for worrying about me."

The coolness in her eyes softened. She leaned in and kissed the corner of his mouth. "Don't forget the barbecue chips."

Claire woke at 4:00 a.m. on day five, rolled her sleeping bag, and stumbled outside to her dogs. Dillon and his team were gone. Powder-fine snow continued to fall in the predawn darkness. Eight new inches covered the sled bag and turned her dogs, curled under their blankets on beds of straw, into breathing mounds with ears.

The peaceful stillness, void of air traffic, made her think of Christmas. A string of multicolored lights hung from the eaves of a cabin at the end of the street. In place of the soft jingle of sleigh bells, the muffled drone of a snow machine drifted from across the river. The thermometer outside the laundromat read minus two degrees as she prepared to feed her team one more time before heading out. Though she was still a little fuzzy from exhaustion, the layover had recharged her and she was ready to move on. Surviving Happy River and Dalzell Gorge left her confident she and her team could make it all the way to Nome.

Fluffy, deep snow slowed travel and increased the odds of moose encounters. She hoped Dillon's run-in was an isolated occurrence, but she would make sure she had easy access to her ax and revolver before leaving McGrath. She hoped dropping Bonnie wouldn't affect Dillon's ability to finish the race.

And she hoped he outdistanced whatever demons rode shotgun with him.

Chapter 17

Maverick's limp worsened on the climb up Porcupine Ridge, and Dillon knew the husky's race was over. Heartsick and plagued by guilt, Dillon loaded him in the sled bag. "I'm sorry, boy." He rested his forehead between the husky's ears. Maverick whimpered and licked Dillon's hand. The dog's utter trust brought tears to Dillon's eyes. It tore him up to let one of his dogs down. *I shouldn't have pushed him.* "Next year," he promised.

He put Clyde in single lead, but the Siberian's heart wasn't in the game. Dillon stopped again. "What's up, man? You missing your sister?" He gave Bonnie's brother a consoling rub. "I don't blame you. I miss her too." Clyde returned to the middle of the team, and Dillon put Deshka in lead. "Let's see how my caramel girl does. You ready for this?"

Deshka's enthusiasm got them to Takotna shortly after 3:00 a.m. Dillon arranged Maverick's drop, loaded a bale of straw, and forced himself to keep moving. From Takotna, the trail followed an old mining road to Ophir and the last remnant of civilization—a 1930s cabin belonging to a couple who flew out every year to help man the checkpoint. Lantern light in the window welcomed the teams.

Clyde lost interest in running, and the rest of the dogs began either pushing or pulling him to force him to keep up. He also stopped eating. Dillon made the tough decision to drop him; as much as he hated to do it, there was no point dragging the inconsolable guy all the way to Nome.

He began the long, isolated stretch to Cripple with thirteen dogs in harness. In minus thirty degrees under a clearing sky, they traveled an easy trail of low rolling hills, creek crossings, and sparse vegetation. By midmorning, each hill and creek looked like the next. They camped trailside, other teams passing them as Dillon checked and fed dogs. Once they were comfortable and sleeping, he rolled his bag out on a bed of straw to grab some downtime for himself. As exhaustion pulled him toward unconsciousness, he thought of Claire's concern and his bullheaded insistence that he'd be all right.

Two hours later, he thrashed awake shouting, "No!"

As midnight approached on day six, Claire cranked the volume on her MP3 player, hoping the noise would keep her lucid. She rocked with the Bee Gees to "Stayin' Alive," belting out made-up lyrics. "Yeah, yeah, yeah, yeah, stayin' awake, stayin' awake. Hey!" she shouted to her dogs, "We're stayin' awake!"

They panted along, keeping pace with the beat.

"Huh, huh, huh, huh," Claire grunted, "stayin' awake, stayin' awake."

As the song faded, staying awake began to feel like too much work. The next song began, a heart-tugging ballad by Eric Clapton. The mix was her own—she preferred older tunes over the newer stuff. Her head drooped and her eyelids drifted shut. *Just a few seconds,* she thought. *What can it hurt?* Her body relaxed forward over the handlebar as Clapton's low, soothing voice sang her to sleep.

The sled dipped and she jerked upright. Her headlamp flashed on a steel cable stretched neck high across the trail, coming straight at her.

Power line!

She ducked hard and slammed her forehead on the handlebar. The MP3 buds popped from her ears, cutting off Clapton midnote. "Ow, shit!" She winced at the explosion of pain across her skull. "What maniac put that there?" Tears sprang to her eyes. "Whoa! Please. Whoa."

The dogs stopped and looked back.

To her amazement, her headlamp was still intact. She twisted around and shined the light on the trail behind her, hoping to spot the guilty culprit lurking in the dark. "You could kill somebody!" she shouted hotly. "You know that, don't you?"

The only response she got was the angry pounding of her pulse in her ears. She swiped at the tears blurring her vision and squinted into the night. Nothing but empty trail and trees. "Coward!" she yelled. "Don't think you can get away with this! I know the law!" *Whoever's responsible will pay,* she vowed. In the meantime, she should mark the cable so other mushers would see it.

Setting the hook, she pulled half a dozen fluorescent dog booties from the bag and walked back down the trail. She went several yards before she realized there was no cable. Lots of trees and snow. No maniac and no cable. An uneasy feeling came over Claire. "Oh man."

She'd heard stories of mushers imagining things that weren't there: sweeping tree limbs on a treeless stretch of trail, roaming elephants, mysterious lights and buildings on sea ice, a train whistle when the nearest tracks were hundreds of miles away. The hallucinations were brought on by exhaustion and dehydration. It shook Claire's confidence. *I'm losing it.*

She returned to her team and pulled up the hook. "Sorry, guys. Let's go. Hike."

Handsome and Ranger got the team moving. As if sensing a need to reach the next checkpoint before their driver went any crazier, they picked up speed.

"Take it easy," Claire said. "What's the hurry?"

And that's when she spotted the glimmer of lights in the distance. She blinked several times to convince herself she wasn't seeing stars from the smack to her forehead. The lights grew larger: the Ruby checkpoint.

"Good dogs!" she called, and winced. "Straight on! Ow."

They would take their first mandatory eight-hour rest at the former gold-rush town with its streets tiered into a cozy bowl along the river. After the marathon run from Ophir to Cripple to Ruby, she and her dogs had covered 495 miles and were in twenty-fourth position, too late to claim the seven-course gourmet meal and cash prize for the First

Musher to the Yukon Award. But volunteers kept a smorgasbord going, including local favorites like moose stew and salmon.

When Claire checked in, she discovered she had missed Dillon by half an hour. *Good. He's still in the race.*

Chapter 18

From Ruby, the Iditarod Trail traveled along the frozen, snow-covered Yukon River. The next checkpoint was Galena, fifty miles away, and then Nulato after another forty miles. Claire and her team were somewhere between Galena and Nulato when the setting sun bled brilliant red and orange across the horizon. "Isn't that the most gorgeous thing you've ever seen?" she called out to her dogs. Picking up on her enthusiasm, they trekked along as though eager to reach it before it disappeared.

Almost two miles wide in places, the Yukon's vastness commanded awe. Chunks of pack ice interrupted an other-wise flat surface bordered on the right by a low range of mountains. Claire ski poled to help her dogs maintain their speed and to lessen the bite of the thirty-below air frosting the fur rim of her parka hood. The temperature seemed to drop another ten degrees when they passed through the shadows cast by the high bank. Thankfully, they had the wind at their backs.

Watching the sun dip low and the colors wane, Claire decided this moment alone made the whole Iditarod experience worth it. "How about it, guys? Does it get any better than this?"

In the pause between sunset and nightfall, she saw what looked like steam rising from the river ice in the distance. She stared for long seconds, thinking it might be another hallucination. Her forehead still smarted from the power line delusion. But the steam remained steady, reminiscent of Bagby Hot Springs in Mount Hood National Forest.

"What on earth?" The dogs' ears stood up. Claire understood their skittish curiosity. Ice should not steam. And there certainly weren't any hot springs out here. The trail appeared to head straight for it. "Easy, guys."

As they got closer, she saw the slice of open water to the left of the trail markers. The cold river water was condensing as it hit the colder air above it, creating the steam cloud. "Would you look at that," Claire said. "Hold up. I need to get a picture."

At 3:30 in the afternoon of day seven, Dillon and his team left Kaltag, the last checkpoint on the Yukon River. Here the

northern and southern routes converged and headed south-west to Unalakleet, eighty-five miles away. They had traveled the frozen river for almost two days. Now the trail followed an ancient portage and marked the transition from inland river to the coast of the Bering Sea. The first fifteen miles climbed through wooded country to an 800-foot summit. Dillon took it slow and pedaled often. Each passing mile made it easier to compartmentalize the nightmares. *Get on with the race. Shake it off.* He made caring for his team his sole focus.

"How's it going, Deshka? You like being in front, don't you? Elliot, you keeping everybody on their toes?"

By nightfall, they'd navigated the descent to Tripod Flats. Dillon opted to rest at the BLM cabin a hundred yards off the trail. He fixed his dogs a hot meal, boiled a bag of beef wieners and chili for himself, and managed to catch an hour of nightmare-free sleep before another team arrived. He'd take what he could get, but he knew it was only a matter of time before sleep deprivation caught up with him.

From the cabin, the trail ran across low hills and ridges on the south side of the Unalakleet River, then along the sloughs of the Old Woman River. Fifteen miles later, they passed the original Old Woman Cabin, said to be haunted by the woman who had lived there years before and died checking her traps. Her body was never found. On his last trip through, Dillon had heard a female voice singing an indecipherable song. This time, he left a candy bar peace offering, just in case there was any truth to the stories of being haunted by bad luck if you didn't. Though in disrepair, the old cabin still served as a shelter when needed.

The trail emerged onto open tundra, and the BLM sign for the new Old Woman Cabin came into sight. Half a dozen teams were parked in the clearing. Dillon didn't want to share an overheated cabin with a bunch of other mushers, so he drove his team a short while longer and found a cluster of straggly trees he could use as shelter against the tundra's pervasive wind while he rested and snacked his dogs.

In the darkness of early morning, they pushed on. His headlamp spotlighted the backs of his dogs as they ran into an endless void. He missed Claire—missed her smile, her laugh, the easy way she had of making him feel wanted. The hours and miles blurred. He faded in and out of consciousness until staying on the sled became his greatest challenge. A moose appeared at light's edge, head down, ready to charge. His dogs motored on as though the beast didn't exist.

Because it didn't. Dillon knew this, yet when he saw another moose lurking in the shadows some time later, he shouted, "Whoa!"

The dogs stopped. Deshka looked back, waiting for instructions. Dillon shined his headlamp over both sides of the trail. Nothing. No sound but the impatient woofs of his team.

"Sorry, kids. Let's go."

The dogs ran on, the rhythm of their gait hypnotic. He thought he saw the green-and-white flash of Unalakleet's airport beacon but couldn't be sure. He felt himself nodding off again and jerked. The beam of his headlamp cut a swath mid-gangline and picked up splotches of red in the tracks of his dogs. He stared for long seconds, his exhausted brain struggling to make sense of something incomprehensible. It looked like blood. *Is one of my dogs hurt?*

With the team churning it up, he couldn't tell. "Whoa!"

The dogs stopped again. He set the hook and walked the gangline, shining his light on each dog's paw. No obvious injuries. Pete lacked a right front bootie. Dillon squatted to examine the exposed paw. His headlamp caught the bloody print of a thumb and forefinger in the snow inches away. His stomach jumped into his throat.

Straightening, he swung his headlamp in a wild arc. A dark figure knelt in the middle of the trail in front of the team, hands planted in stains of blood. Recognition tore through Dillon. He swallowed against the urge to vomit. The figure's head came up, and Dillon's lamp shined full in the eyes of a dead man.

Chapter 19

Just before noon, Claire arrived at the Unalakleet checkpoint in time to catch Dillon in the process of packing to leave. "Hey!" she called as volunteers led her team to a parking spot a few yards away.

He walked over. "Hey yourself."

The spooked look she'd seen on his face at McGrath had returned. She masked her concern behind a tired smile. "Tough run?" she asked.

He expelled a heavy breath. "The hallucinations are hell."

Claire smirked and lifted her hood to expose the goose egg on her forehead. "Tell me about it. I ducked a power line that wasn't there coming into Ruby."

"Ouch." He leaned in and brushed his chapped lips against the edge of the bruise.

"What about you?" she asked when he pulled back.

"It's not important."

"That bad, huh?"

He didn't answer.

Claire shrugged to cover the sting of his unwillingness to talk. "Well, I'd better get my dogs taken care of," she said, and turned away to grab a snub line.

Dillon took her arm and coaxed her to face him. When she did, his haunted eyes implored her to understand. "If I don't talk about it," he said, his words measured, "then it's not important."

She understood. She knew how it felt to carry a wound so deep that locking it inside was the only way to deal with it. And she understood the destructive consequences of keeping it locked inside to fester.

Lifting her chin, she pressed her mouth to his. It was like kissing a snowman wearing medicated lip balm. "When you're ready to talk, I'm ready to listen."

He gave a brief nod. "Take care of yourself out there."

"You too."

A ground blizzard drove snow and ice sideways through the narrow wind tunnel of the Kwik River Valley, obliterating the trail. It tore at the little warmth remaining in Claire's exhausted limbs and scoured the exposed areas of her face with gales of pellets like coarse sand.

"Hey there, Zach," she shouted through her neck gaiter, "how're you doing? Riley, you still with us? How're Pepper and Trouble doing up there?"

They had endured frigid, gusting winds on the barren coastline from Unalakleet to Shaktoolik, crossed pressure ridges serenaded by the unnerving sound of cracking sea ice over Norton Bay to Koyuk, and finally headed inland, hoping to make the Elim checkpoint before dark. If they kept moving, they'd make it.

As evening neared, the wind and cold weren't her only enemies. Fatigue made every move and decision an effort in determination. Talking to her dogs helped her stay awake, if not alert. Her mind was obsessed with the thing it needed most—a good night's sleep—while her body just tried to survive.

Her goggles frosted over. She swiped at the lens, but they frosted again within minutes. She lost sight of the trail markers, lost sight of Handsome and Ranger, then Toolik and Treker.

Are we even going in the right direction anymore?

She pulled her goggles off and attempted to peer through the fur-lined edge of her hood. Ice crystals formed on her lashes and froze her right eye shut. She rubbed at it with her mitten and put her goggles back on. Unless the wind had changed direction, they were still headed toward Elim. She hoped.

The trail across frozen Golovnin Lagoon ran straight and monotonous. After the slow grind over Little McKinley and an icy descent into the wind of the bay between Elim and Golovin, Dillon let his dogs set the pace. He pedaled at the back of the sled as an endless stream of trail markers led the way toward the flashing airport beacon of the White Mountain checkpoint—seventy-seven miles from Nome—where they'd take their second mandatory eight-hour layover. His face numbed by the wind that blew down the river, he felt caught in a time warp, his dogs running in slow motion, the beacon like a mirage in the desert, never getting any closer.

As the afternoon lengthened, tedium set in and his mind drifted. He didn't want to think about the dead man but did anyway. He'd thought himself purged of the memory, or at least thought he had buried it deep enough. But claustrophobia shadowed him, tried to trap him in a room he swore to never enter again. A room of nightmares and flashbacks and chaos.

Shake it off, damn it.

He realized his dogs had picked up their pace and the airport beacon was no longer a distant mirage. Checkpoints meant food and rest and attention from the locals, three items high on a dog's list of things to get excited about. They swung around a bend and saw White Mountain spread out along the bank of the river. Dillon checked in at 5:21 p.m., loaded his dropped bags onto the sled, and followed the volunteer to the parking area. He went through the routine of feeding and bedding his team for the long stay as the sun set and darkness settled in.

Later, he walked to the community hall in search of a hot meal. While he enjoyed a bowl of stew, he overheard a group of mushers talking about a ground blizzard between Koyuk and Elim—minus twenty-eight degrees, fifty-mile-an-hour winds.

"Nobody's getting through there," one commented.

"Anybody caught in it?" Dillon asked.

"Maybe," a woman with loose dark hair and sleep-droopy eyelids replied. "That rookie lawyer should have checked in at Elim by now, but nobody's seen her."

Dillon's spoon stopped partway to his mouth as a sudden uncomfortable knot formed in his throat. "You mean Claire Stanfield?"

"Yeah, that's the one."

"What's her GPS tracker say?"

"It's not moving."

Chapter 20

A maelstrom of white assaulted Claire as she searched for the reflection of a trail marker in the light of her headlamp. She needed to find shelter for herself and her dogs. There was supposed to be a cabin twenty-five miles from Elim, but she feared she could be standing right next to it and not see it. The longer they blindly thrashed on, the greater the odds of getting lost. If they weren't already. What if the wind had shifted? What if they'd been going in circles?

Can you be strong for me?

"Mama?" The wind ripped the question from her mouth, scattering it like confetti. "Mama, is that you?"

Oh God, I'm hallucinating again. The thought sent a jag of panic through her. How could she take care of her dogs if she couldn't trust what she was seeing or hearing?

They'd have to stop now, cabin or no cabin.

"Whoa!"

The dogs didn't need any further encouragement. Setting the snow hook, Claire made her way forward, shining her light on each dog, calling names as she went—Sugar, Daisy, Harmony, Sam. Putting the right name to the right dog helped her focus. Ginny, Mama's Boy, Zach. They wore their jackets against the heat-sucking wind. She checked ties and snaps, straightened and tightened where needed, checked booties, and wiped a mitten over frosted faces.

She reached the front of her team. "How's my Handsome man?" He cast her a doleful look as she deiced his face. The poor guy had been taking the brunt of the weather, running lead with Ranger. He'd clearly had enough. Another jag of panic, stronger this time. Handsome was her rock. What would she do if he quit on her?

She looked to his running mate and wiped ice from the little dog's mask. "How's my Lone Ranger doing? You've been here before. Any idea where that cabin is?"

The wind howled, but the undaunted husky tossed his head and leaned into his harness as if eager to go. Matt had told her Ranger was her best bet in blizzard conditions. She didn't fully appreciate that fact until she squinted in the direction the dog pointed and the light from her headlamp flashed across the board siding of a cabin. She blinked and looked again.

His dogs slept. He needed sleep too. As he paced and waited, every step took a monumental effort—every action a long, deliberate process. The Iditarod volunteer he questioned said Claire left Koyuk ten hours ago. Under normal conditions, that stretch of trail should have taken five to seven. She could be stopped at a shelter cabin, but there was no way to know for sure. Stopped could also mean waiting out the blizzard trailside just yards from a cabin she didn't see. Dillon knew she could take care of herself, but he also knew how bad things could go for even the most experienced musher. Lead dogs tended to turn downwind if visibility was poor or if they had lost the trail markers, taking the team onto shore ice and toward open water. Wind accelerated dehydration in both dogs and humans, leading to muscle cramps, light-headedness, weakness—heart failure. Frostbite could set in. Snow blindness. Hypothermia.

Dillon couldn't shake the endless cycle of concern that kept him from the rest his body cried for. "Damn it, Claire. Where are you?"

He vowed to tell her everything. No more secrets. *Just let her be safe.*

The sun warmed her face and made her head itchy. She loved August and digging up weeds, watering the tomatoes, and picking lemon cucumbers. The cucumber leaves prickled her hands as she moved them back to see what they might be hiding. There, plump and round and dark yellow on top. She pinched the cucumber from the vine, rubbed the tiny black spines off with her fingers, and took a bite. Mama had her head under the green beans draping from the tall trellis, just her red shorts and tan legs showing. Mama had beautiful legs. Daddy said so all the time.

"Honey, empty the colander for me, please?" Mama called.

"Okay." She ran barefoot between the grow boxes of lettuce and spinach and took the colander full of green beans from her mama's outstretched hand. As she turned toward the picnic table, she stuck a long bean in her mouth and snapped the crisp skin between her teeth.

Mama laughed, her head still hidden under the vines. "No wonder you're not hungry at mealtime."

She liked the sound of Mama's laugh, like bells tinkling. A big bowl already half full of green beans waited on the picnic table. Another bowl was filled with cherry tomatoes. She took one and popped it into her cheek, then took another one and popped it into her other cheek. Chipmunk cheeks.

"I need that colander back," Mama called. "Did you get lost?"

She giggled. *Silly Mama. You can't get lost in your own garden.* "I'm coming!"

I'm not lost…

Claire woke. Not in the garden but in darkness. The taste of cherry tomatoes lingered in her mouth. She reached for her headlamp and turned it on. After securing her dogs and sled on the sheltered side of the cabin, she had spread out her sleeping bag inside and fallen asleep.

"I'm not lost," she said to the quiet.

Silence answered her.

"The wind's stopped." She flung back her sleeping bag and shoved her feet into icy boots. Time to get back in the race. *I'm coming, Mama!*

"You're the guy sweet on that lady lawyer, aren't you?"

Dillon looked up from smearing salve on Rocky's paw. He recognized the musher standing over him as one of the two who'd ribbed him for shaving at McGrath. "Has there been news?"

The musher grinned through his shaggy moustache. "Looks like you're gonna need to dig that razor out. She and her team made it to Elim safe and sound."

Chapter 21

Fifty-five miles separated White Mountain from the Safety checkpoint. The trail climbed barren, exposed ridges, ran along twelve miles of the shore's driftwood line subject to eighty-mile-an-hour gales and whiteouts, and moved through a series of natural wind tunnels, localized and violent, called "blow holes." It was a stretch of trail that could make or break a musher within a few hours of reaching Nome.

Dillon knew this, and as he prepped his team to leave the White Mountain checkpoint, he was more conscious than ever of the weather report: calm conditions. At 1:21 a.m., he and his dogs headed out, ending their final mandatory stop.

As they emerged from the shelter of the hill behind White Mountain, a place where north winds were common, the weather report proved accurate. The wind remained calm until the descent onto the Topkok River, where they hit glare ice and twenty-mile-per-hour gusts blasted them sideways. Dillon wrestled into his wind jacket and turned his headlamp on to locate the reflective tripod markers. He didn't see any and realized the wind had pushed them off course, toward open water. "Gee, Deshka! Gee!"

Behind him bobbed the headlamps of three other mushers, pinpricks of light dancing in the distance. Dillon knew their dogs would follow the scent of his. He didn't want to be responsible for leading them off the trail. *Where the hell are the markers?*

The wind continued to pummel them, and time slowed. Dillon couldn't be sure they were headed in the right direction. A thread of panic wormed its way into his thoughts. He considered stopping and waiting for one of the teams behind them to catch up. Maybe one of the other mushers knew something he didn't.

Then he spotted it: the reflection of a marker. "Come gee!" he called, but it was unnecessary. The dogs had already picked up the smell and altered course.

Two hours later, the gusts let up and one headlamp caught and passed Dillon's team. In his wind-battered exhaustion, he couldn't tell who the musher was. The other two teams had dropped back.

The weather held as they traveled the driftwood line separating them from the sea ice and open water. The moon came out, bathing the vast shore in a ghostly white radiance. Dillon turned off his headlamp. As his dogs ran, nostalgia set in. He was almost home, almost to the place where he'd taken refuge. Nome, Alaska, was as close to heaven as he figured he'd ever get. He wanted to share it with Claire. He wanted to give whatever they had together a chance to grow. But there was the promise she'd made to her dad.

And she would expect total honesty from him.

The whole truth, and nothing but the truth.

Talking about his past would open a door he didn't want to go through. The beast he'd locked up had already begun pushing its way out, pushing against its years of solitary confinement. He didn't know how much longer he could keep it contained. The beast scared him.

But losing Claire scared him more.

Moonlight had given way to sunrise when Dillon and his team reached the Safety checkpoint. He treated his dogs to a quick snack and put on his bib for the final twenty-two miles to Nome. The dogs sensed home and didn't waste any time getting back on the trail.

"You know where we're at, don't you, Deshka?" Her ears flicked at the sound of her name. "Guy, you old hound. I bet you're dreaming of a cushy nap!"

They followed Nome-Council Road past Cape Nome, where they encountered moderate wind at their backs before cutting down to the beach. The light towers of the airport blinked in the distance. Two miles out, Dillon heard the fire department siren announce their approach.

"Almost there, kids!"

They swung up a ramp with life-size gnome cutouts holding signs that read, "Mush ahead to a warm bed," and "There's no place like Nome." *Amen to that,* Dillon thought. "Haw!"

The team turned left onto Front Street and headed for the burled arch half a mile away. A white police vehicle, red-and-blue lights flashing, escorted them to the finish chute, where Dillon spotted Frank waiting. He'd know that wild red hair and beard anywhere.

"Welcome back!" Frank hollered.

"Thanks! How's Bonnie?"

Frank fell into a trot alongside the sled. "She's doing good. Mav too. 'Course, Clyde perked up as soon as he saw his sister."

People lined the fenced chute for the final couple hundred feet. Some called him by name—neighbors, shop owners, people who he was sure he knew but who his tired brain couldn't place. Deshka passed under the burled arch, and Dillon stopped the sled. Time: 11:31 a.m. They'd finished the race in ten days, twenty hours, and thirty-one minutes, placing twenty-third. It was a bittersweet accomplishment for Dillon, his relief and satisfaction overshadowed by the fact that he could no longer run away from his demons.

A checker congratulated him, pulling him back into the moment, and began to inventory his gear, including the symbolic letter. Volunteers held his sled so he could walk the length of his team and give each dog an ear rub or a pat on the head. "Good job, Pete. That's my Blackie. There's Elliot with energy to spare." When he got to Deshka, he dropped to his knees in the snow and wrapped his arms around the husky's neck. "I couldn't have done it without you, girl." She licked his frosted cheek.

He stood and saw Janey and Andy. The boy gave him a hug that challenged his worn-out legs. "You made it!"

"Hey, sport."

Janey beamed. "Congratulations. Matt wanted to be here, but somebody had to look after things at home."

"Thanks for coming." Dillon swallowed the lump in his

throat, feeling stupid for getting emotional. He blamed it on fatigue. "It's good to be home."

Janey pulled the man standing behind her forward. He looked uncomfortable in his new arctic gear, bundled up so tight only his face showed. To someone who'd come off the frozen sea ice moments earlier, Nome's seven degrees felt balmy, but Dillon figured the man didn't want to hear that. *He belongs in an expensive suit commanding the attention of a judge and jury in a city where it rains a lot.*

Dillon's intuition proved correct when Janey made introductions.

"Dillon Cord, this is Ethan Stanfield, Claire's father."

Mr. Stanfield extended his gloved hand. "Congratulations on finishing the race."

He had a firm grip, even through thick layers of insulation. "Thank you, sir. Welcome to Nome. I need to take care of my dogs and get a shower, but come by the Bering West later and I'll buy you a drink."

The older man hunched farther into his parka like a turtle drawing into its shell. "Make that a *hot* drink and you've got a deal."

The dogs were taken down the street to a team of veterinarians for a thorough checkup, during which a drug-testing team took urine samples. Then Dillon and Frank trucked the dogs home to Frank's kennel yard to eat and rest.

He should have been dead on his feet, ready to curl up like his team of athletes and sleep for twenty hours, but Dillon's system was still on race time—run, rest, feed, check feet, repeat. Now nothing stood between him and his bed over the Bering West.

Except Claire was still out there on the trail.

And he had to buy a man a drink. He wasn't sure what

had compelled him to make the offer. Did he hope to influence Mr. Stanfield in some way? Convince him his daughter should stay in Alaska?

Maybe he just wanted to meet the guy Claire held dear to her heart.

Chapter 22

Dillon couldn't say what he expected Claire's dad to be like—a hard-nosed tyrant, a money-hungry suit, an iron-fisted bully. But none of those clichés fit the man who walked into the Bering West and sat at the bar later that afternoon. Most of the tables were occupied even at midday because of Iditarod activities around town. The young couple at the bar were tourists from Minnesota. Marty Robbins sang "El Paso" on the jukebox, and the aroma of fresh-ground coffee beans mingled with the pervasive smell of hops.

Frank started over to take Ethan Stanfield's order. "I've got this," Dillon said, then turned to his guest. "Glad you could make it. What'll it be?"

"Coffee, please. Black and strong." Stanfield unbuttoned his parka and swiveled on the barstool to take in his surroundings. "You have an interesting place here, Mr. Cord."

Dillon had done his best to replicate an Old West saloon. Decks of cards on round wood tables surrounded by an assortment of straight-backed chairs invited the occasional poker game. A brass boot rail ran the length of the polished bar. Behind the bar, a long etched mirror reflected rows of liquor bottles. Some might question a man with Dillon's history owning a tavern—that is, if anyone knew his history. But he saw it as a testament to himself that he'd put his drinking days behind him.

"The tourists like it," he said, and tossed two coasters with the logo of a compass pointing west onto the bar. He set a thick ironstone mug on each and nodded toward the historical photographs of Nome. "People still migrate here after the thaw to pan for gold."

Stanfield pulled deeper into his parka. "It would take more than the illusive chance of striking it rich on a chunk of mineral for me to vacation this close to the Arctic, no matter what time of year. No offense."

"None taken." Dillon shrugged. "It's not bad once the sea ice thaws."

The older man barked a laugh. "Good God." He lifted the coffee Dillon had poured. "What makes a man choose to live in such a bleak, isolated place?"

You're not welcome in this house. "The isolation."

"One man's harsh and bleak is another man's safe haven." Stanfield took a sip and gave a long sigh.

Dillon returned the carafe and sipped from his own mug. Strong and hot. "Couldn't get enough of this on the trail."

"What's it like out there?"

He saw the concern of a parent in Stanfield's eyes. But if the man was anything like his daughter, a sugarcoated answer wouldn't fly. "I can tell you it was forty below with a windchill factor that made it feel like minus eighty, but until you've experienced it, those are just numbers." There were no words to describe the overwhelming, harsh conditions. The sleep deprivation. The hallucinations. "When you're in it, all you think about is surviving. And when it's over, you're already planning the next race."

Stanfield's head came up, his gaze sharp. "No."

"Sir?"

"I can't go through this again."

"Is that why you made Claire promise to return to Portland?"

Gravity pulled at the man's face. "Her idea, not mine." He lifted his mug and paused before drinking, as though giving himself time to choose his next words. "Did she tell you anything about her mother?"

"No, sir."

"My wife, Caroline, had cancer. Very aggressive cancer. Claire was eleven when her mother went in for a risky surgical procedure. Caroline promised our daughter she'd see her again soon—a promise she wasn't able to keep."

"It must have been hard on both of you."

"Terrifying," Stanfield admitted. "I lost the only woman I'd ever loved and suddenly found myself with an eleven-year-old girl to raise on my own. I made a lot of mistakes, but we survived. And since her mother's death, Claire has been unyielding, to the point of obsession, about keeping promises."

"She didn't want you to feel abandoned."

Stanfield nodded and sipped his coffee.

Dillon saw the man's hand shake and looked away. Jealousy

dug at him. A jealousy he had no right to feel. He had nobody but himself to blame for the break in his relationship with his parents. Still, he couldn't stop himself from saying, "You didn't try to talk her out of it."

"I won't lie, I would miss her. But my daughter's good at what she does. Better than good. I'd hate to see her give it up for..." He hesitated. Tammy Wynette belted "Stand by Your Man," and he sighed. "Less."

Dillon should have taken offense, but he understood where the man was coming from. And with that understanding came the knowledge that he would not be the one to get between Claire and her dad. Where that left him in the equation, he didn't have a clue.

"Have I answered your question, Mr. Cord?"

"Yes, sir." He reached for the carafe. "Refill?"

"Thank you, but no." Stanfield stood and buttoned his parka. "I've kept you long enough. You must be exhausted."

Dillon shook the man's hand. "It was a pleasure. Claire will be happy to see you."

"Stunned is more like it. Maybe a game of poker later?"

"Not if you're the one who taught Claire how to play."

Stanfield grinned. "How much did she take you for?"

"A box of matches."

"Well, I can assure you, your odds are better with me. I taught my daughter the basics of the game, but the finer points she figured out for herself. I suppose I can take somewhat dubious comfort in knowing that if she gets tired of being an attorney, she can support herself as a card shark."

Dillon chuckled. "I don't doubt that."

Chapter 23

Shortly after 5:30 the next morning, Claire and her dogs rounded the corner onto Front Street. In the predawn darkness, strands of lights overhead illuminated the chute in festive bursts of red, blue, and green. People clapped and cheered as Claire stopped her team under the burled arch. She was exhausted, cold, and grinning wide enough to crack the ice on her face.

"Welcome to Nome," the checker said.

"Thank you," she beamed. A man bundled in a new parka and ski pants approached. Claire blinked in disbelief. "Daddy?"

"Peanut." He staggered at the force of her hug. "You've lost weight," he said, patting her back with a concerned frown.

She pressed wind-chapped lips to his cheek, and he gasped. "God, you're an ice cube!"

She laughed through the tears that sprang to her eyes. "It's so wonderful to see you, Daddy."

"You too, peanut. Wonderful, and a relief."

Guilt tugged at Claire over the anxiety she had caused him, but an apology felt out of place in the midst of the high she was riding. No sooner did she step out of her dad's arms than Janey and Andy embraced her in a double bear hug. Claire sagged into them as the enormity of what she'd just accomplished weakened her knees.

"Whoa," Janey chuckled and steadied her. "Are you okay?"

Claire pulled away and squealed, "I did it!"

"You did it!" Janey squealed in return.

Claire scanned the crowd for Dillon, and Janey pointed to the balcony of a two-story wood building a few yards away: the Bering West. Claire's heart tripped when she recognized Dillon standing at the railing. He gave her two thumbs up and she waved.

"He's treating us all to breakfast later," Janey commented. "Anything we want, he said."

Claire was sure the rush of warmth up her neck would melt the ice crystals clinging to her cheeks. She turned away and got to the business of thanking her dogs, completing her check-in, and getting her team settled in the dog yard. Her official time was eleven days, fourteen hours, and eight minutes. She had finished her first Iditarod in twenty-seventh place.

During the Iditarod, Nome's population of 3,500 swelled by 1,000 or more. People from all over the world converged on the town, looking for an opportunity to rub shoulders with famous mushers and taking part in dozens of events— fine art and Native craft shows, sing-alongs, IditaRides, IditaShoots, helicopter tours, and hoedowns—that combined to bring the "Mardi Gras of the North" to the coastal city.

And all those people needed to eat. Dillon donned an apron and began mixing a massive batch of pancake batter while Vic prepped tomatoes, onions, and ham for country scrambled eggs. A breakfast crowd—both tourists and regulars—had already begun to form outside.

"It's been like this all week," Vic groused, his knife rapping the cutting board like a woodpecker on caffeine. He'd pulled his long gray-streaked hair into a braid at his back, his thick arms bare to the shoulders, exposing the tattoo of a woman's name—Reta—on his right bicep.

Dillon didn't have a clue who Reta was or had been. He was curious, but not curious enough to risk stirring up bitter feelings over a failed relationship. He respected the man's privacy. "You love it," he said, to which his cook gave a boisterous hoot. "The Iditarod is good for business."

"Good enough for a raise?"

"Dream on."

Damn, it felt good to be home. Comfortable. The routine, the bantering, the constant workload. There was nothing wrong with falling back on routine while deciding what the hell to do next.

Helen and Kristi swung into action as soon as the doors opened, showing people to tables and taking orders.

"Order!" Helen bellowed. Then she turned to Dillon and

asked in a loud whisper, "So, who's the looker at table two?" Just about everything the woman did was at a low roar.

Dillon had reserved table two for Claire and her group. He knew which one of the bunch he'd choose as "the looker" but doubted it was the same one Helen had her eye on. "You'll have to be more specific."

"Nice build, gorgeous gray hair. About my age."

Helen's age was vague at best. Dillon knew she had at least ten years on the forty she had put on her job application, but he had let it slide. Helen knew how to waitress, and customers liked her. That was all he cared about. "Name's Ethan Stanfield," he said. "He's an attorney from Portland, Oregon."

"Is he spoken for?"

"Not that I'm aware of." The conversation he'd had with Claire's dad yesterday afternoon led him to believe the man still mourned his deceased wife. He figured his brash, outspoken employee had as much chance of attracting Stanfield as a moose had of flying, but what did he know? His own experience in love didn't count for much.

Helen grinned and waggled her eyebrows.

"Be nice," Dillon told her.

"Aren't I always?"

Dillon chuckled. "You don't really want me to answer that, do you?"

"Hell no!"

A few minutes later, he turned toward the pick-up counter with a loaded plate of food in each hand and stopped just short of colliding with Claire.

"Whoa! Sorry," she said, taking a quick step back.

But not so quick he didn't have time to plant a kiss on her forehead before she got out of range. "Good morning." He set the plates on the counter. "Orders up!" He turned back and saw Claire standing to the side, looking uncertain. Tired, but irresistible.

"Helen said it was okay. If I'm—"

He pulled her close, whispered, "It's okay," and kissed her full on the mouth. She tasted of coffee with a dollop of Claire for sweetness.

"I missed you," she said on a breath.

His heart drummed. "I missed you too." He kissed her again. Deeper. The uncertainty of tomorrow warned him to go slow, but that was damn near impossible when she was pressed against him, warm and smelling of pine soap.

A wolf whistle pierced the air.

Dillon flinched, felt Claire's smile on his mouth. He eased his hold with a sigh and shot a glare at Helen.

She winked, picked up the orders, and sauntered off.

Still looking amused, Claire commented, "I thought cooking was one of those things you sucked at."

"It is!" Vic hollered.

"I can hold my own in the kitchen."

Vic grunted. "Is that why my sausages are lookin' like desiccated dog turds?"

"Damn it." Dillon made introductions as he scraped burnt links into the garbage. "Claire, this is Vic. Vic, Claire."

Vic flashed her a grin. "Charmed, darlin'."

Claire gave a smile and a quick wave. "Nice to meet you." She moved toward the door. "I'd better let you get back to... cooking."

Dillon shot her a smile. "Catch you later?"

"Absolutely."

The dining area of the Bering West consisted of half a dozen booths and eight tables, every one of them occupied. The combination of gnarled polished wood and red vinyl gave it a homey atmosphere that Claire found appealing. Sepia photographs of bearded prospectors and their pack mules hung beside tarnished gold pans and pickaxes—testaments to Nome's history as a booming mining town. Batwing doors reminiscent of a Dodge City saloon separated the bar from the restaurant.

A young woman who looked barely out of high school worked one end of the dining area, her blond ponytail swinging behind her, while the woman who introduced herself as Helen worked the side where Claire, her dad, Janey, and Andy were seated. Helen was the one who had invited Claire to go back to the kitchen when Claire asked about Dillon, then whistled when she caught them kissing. She had short auburn curls cut in a no-nonsense, easy-care style and eyes that welcomed friends and strangers alike with equal warmth, yet missed nothing. A pink flannel shirt and blue jeans complemented her mature curves. She moved with confidence as she laid out enormous plates of pancakes, scrambled eggs, bacon, and sausage, milk for Andy, and all the coffee the adults could drink.

Claire knew her brain was fuzzy from lack of sleep, but there was no mistaking the way Helen leaned in slightly and took extra care as she filled her dad's cup. "Would you like sugar and cream with your coffee?" she asked sweetly, giving him a direct look.

"No, I—" He blinked. "Black is fine."

Helen winked and touched his shoulder lightly. "I'll get you some more syrup for those pancakes."

Claire had never seen her dad flustered before. Women had come on to him in the past, of course. After all, he was handsome in a distinguished, business-suit way. Fit, though you couldn't tell with all the ridiculous layers he was wearing to keep warm. He never raised his voice, except on rare occasions to argue a point in court. He was generous, honest, and, at the moment, utterly out of his element.

Claire found it charming. It added another layer to the surreal fog she felt herself floating in—exhausted, yet still riding an adrenaline high.

Janey's eyebrows appeared to be locked in an upright position as she watched the flirtation play out. Claire loved it. A match even her matchmaking friend hadn't predicted.

"More coffee, honey?"

Claire looked up and realized Helen was addressing her. "Yes, please."

Helen gave her a knowing smile and Claire felt her cheeks grow warm. The woman filled her cup and topped off Janey's before sauntering over to Claire's dad. "Anything for dessert?" she asked him.

Claire couldn't have said what it was about the question that implied more than a slice of pie being offered—maybe the uncharacteristic softness in Helen's voice when she said *dessert*—but her dad's face turned as bright as his red flannel shirt.

He cleared his throat and swallowed hard enough for Claire to see his Adam's apple bounce. "Just coffee…for now, thank you."

"A rain check, then?" Helen refilled his cup, not missing a beat.

"I, uh…" He cleared his throat again and cut his eyes in Claire's direction.

Don't look at me! I've got my own love life to figure out. Heat rushed to her face again as she remembered the promise in Dillon's kiss. She glanced away, fearing her dad might see her blush.

"Yes. I'd like that," she heard him tell Helen.

Janey sputtered into her coffee cup. Claire felt her mouth drop open and closed it.

"I'd like some dessert!" Andy announced, clearly annoyed at being left out.

Helen gave a merry laugh. "Of course, sugar. How 'bout a big chocolate chip cookie with a scoop of vanilla ice cream and another glass of milk to wash it down?"

"Yes, please!"

Helen looked to Janey, who nodded. "I'll be right back."

Chapter 24

Dillon worked through the lunch shift before Vic kicked him out. "You're dead on your feet and in my way," Vic grumbled. "I can handle the kitchen 'til Martha's shift. Been doin' it that way the entire time you were out playing with your dogs. I can do it that way a while longer. Besides," he waved a pair of tongs at him, "you look like hell."

Vic was right. Dillon could barely keep his eyes open, and he had royally screwed up that last order. "All right then. Don't disturb me unless the place is on fire." He didn't hear Vic's response as he headed for the back stairway. No need to: he already knew it would be brief and colorful. *Yeah, it's good to be home.*

Once he reached his apartment on the second floor, he made for bed, stumbling out of his shoes on the way. His eyes closed before he felt the pillow beneath his head. He slept deep and hard.

Three hours later, he woke in a cold sweat, the smell of cordite and blood and pizza caught in the back of his throat, his heart hammering against his ribs.

After breakfast, Claire went to the room Janey had reserved for her and slept. She'd almost forgotten how wonderful a real mattress felt: soft, quiet, warm. A few hours later, she woke with a jolt, certain her dogs needed tending. When she realized her mistake, that her adventure was over, sadness had her wrestling to get comfortable.

Then it was time to get up and help Janey and Andy load the dogs in animal carriers for the flight home. Claire hugged and thanked each dog again for getting her to Nome safely. Handsome winked a blue eye at her and she kissed him on the nose. Groucho huffed and immediately curled up to resume his nap. Ginny licked Claire's hand. Claire's heart tightened and her eyes blurred. She'd see them all in a couple days when she flew back to Sommer Kennels after the mushers' banquet, but that didn't stop the tears. Every passing minute brought her time in Alaska closer to an end. It hurt.

Dillon's friend Frank loaned them the use of his truck, and Claire's dad, Janey, and Andy stuffed their luggage around the carriers in the back and piled into the front seat. Claire drove them to Nome Airport, where they'd take a plane to Anchorage.

From there, Janey, Andy, and the dogs would catch a flight to Talkeetna, and Claire's dad would fly back to Portland.

"Don't cry, Auntie Claire," Andy said, throwing his arms around her waist while they waited in the cramped seating area outside the concourse's security gate. "It'll be okay."

"I know it will, hon. I'm just going to miss you," she said as she knelt and kissed his cheek, "a whole bunch."

"You can stay and have my room forever," he offered.

Claire gave a laugh that sounded like a sob. "I appreciate that." Straightening, she hugged her dad. "I'm so glad you were here to see me finish the race."

"I am too, peanut. I'm proud of you."

And once again tears sprang to her eyes. "Thank you, Daddy. Have a safe—"

The glass door to the concourse banged open. "Tell me I haven't missed him!" Helen weaved around a row of seats and rushed at Claire's dad, grabbing his face in her hands and pressing her lips to his. The kiss left them both clinging to each other.

Claire heard Helen whisper, "Don't be a stranger." Her dad's response was too low to make out, but judging by the saucy swing to Helen's hips as she walked away, it must have been what the woman wanted to hear.

"Daddy?"

He gave her a quick sidelong glance before returning his gaze to Helen's retreating figure. Claire hadn't seen such a dopey, contented look in his eyes since...well, since Mama.

"What happened between you two while I was asleep?" she asked.

He quirked a smile. "A gentleman doesn't kiss and tell."

Claire looked at Janey in stunned amusement. "Did you know about this?"

Janey opened her mouth, but it was Andy who answered, "Mom set it up! She said—"

Janey clapped her hand over her son's mouth. "Little boys should mind their own business," she warned, her face bright as an overripe peach.

They were laughing when the Anchorage flight was announced for boarding, but by the time Claire had dispensed another round of hugs and kisses, her tears had returned.

Dillon couldn't get back to sleep and had no desire to even try, so he showered and went in search of Claire.

He didn't have to go far. She and Vic sat at the small table in the corner the kitchen staff used for breaks.

"We were just talking about you," Vic said.

"Explains why my ears are burning. Isn't your shift over?"

"Yep."

And that, apparently, was all the explanation he'd get. Vic stood, leaned in close to Claire, and murmured something for her ears only that made her smile. Then he walked away.

Dillon took Vic's place and reached for Claire's hand across the table. Her fingers twined with his. "How're you doing?" he asked.

She shrugged and gripped his hand tighter, as though clinging to a lifeline. "I knew this day would come. It's just…" Tears pooled in her eyes.

Dillon tugged at her hand and she came to him, let him bundle her into his lap as she buried her face in his collar and quietly cried.

"Have you had any sleep?" he asked.

"A little this morning, until I woke thinking I had a team to feed."

"It'll take a while to get over that."

"How about you? Have you slept?"

"Some. Until the nightmare."

She looked at him. "You ready to talk about it yet?"

He could see how difficult it was for her to ask. Considering his bullheaded silence until now, he didn't blame her. But she deserved to know. Maybe knowing would make it easier for her to say goodbye. "Yes. But not here."

He took her to his loft apartment on the second floor, an open space of tongue-and-groove flooring and varnished wood. An area rug in greens and reds provided a focal point of color, flanked on one side by a double bed with a forest-green quilt and on the other by a kitchen island. Claire spent a moment taking in the comfortable simplicity of the place before her attention was drawn to the broad windows that looked out over Front Street and the Bering Sea.

"God, what a view," she said on a breath. She crossed the room and stepped onto the balcony. Dillon followed. Below, a mass of people were participating in the festivities, with laughter and dozens of conversations going at once. Farther out was the ice of Alaska's west coast. She moved to the railing and inhaled the cold, sharp air redolent of grilled reindeer and woodsmoke. Humans and canines were packed together at the edge of a horizon that stretched on forever. *I could be happy here,* she thought. It brought a twinge of envy. "The sunsets must be stunning."

Dillon leaned with his elbows against the railing, close but not quite touching, looking out to sea. The scruff of beard on his weather-scoured jaw and the compelling line of his mouth were familiar and intimate. "This place keeps me anchored," he said. Those glacier-blue eyes aimed at her then, startling and still so full of secrets.

Sane. This place keeps him sane. She acknowledged the feeling, identified with it.

The fire department siren announced another musher and team coming in. The crowd below cheered and applauded the arrival and Claire joined in, remembering the thrill of finishing. Dillon gave a long, sharp whistle.

"Do you know how many are still on the trail?" Claire asked.

"Maybe a dozen. I stopped counting once you made it in."

"You heard about the blizzard?"

"I was taking my eight at White Mountain when the news came through."

She slid her hands into her jacket pockets and gave an involuntary shiver. "It hit so fast. If Ranger hadn't found that cabin, I don't know what—"

"You did everything right, Claire. You survived and you got your dogs home safe."

Claire's heart ached with a bittersweet combination of accomplishment and sadness. "I'm going to miss them." Dillon nodded his understanding, and her tears returned. She would miss more, much more, than just the dogs. She palmed tears from her face. "Shit."

"You need food."

His declaration startled a laugh from her. "You're right."

They went inside. Claire perched on a cushioned stool at

the kitchen island, facing the white counters, natural wood, and white appliances. It was tidy, with not a single dirty dish in the porcelain sink. Dillon rounded the island and opened a cabinet.

"Need any help?" she asked, though she suspected he knew more about cooking than Vic gave him credit for.

"Got it handled," he said, and pulled out the biggest bag of barbecue potato chips she'd ever seen.

"Oh my God."

He dangled it over the island. "Potato, not corn."

She snagged the bag from him, ripped it open, and stuffed an orange chip in her mouth. "Oh my God," she repeated, her words muffled around the salt and tang of artificially flavored deep-fried potato. She eyed Dillon's slanted smile. "Don't expect me to share."

"I thought I'd open a can of soup."

"Canned soup?"

His smile wavered. "Or we could go—"

"I love canned soup."

He chuckled. "Vegetable beef okay?"

Her stomach growled. "Uh-huh."

They ate side by side at the island. Dillon brewed a pot of coffee. "If you'd like anything stronger, I can run downstairs to the bar."

"Coffee's fine. Alcohol right now would just knock me out. But go for it if you want something."

"I don't drink."

This caught her off guard. "Oh. Okay."

"It's one of the things I left behind when I came to Alaska."

She blew on a spoonful of soup. It tasted wonderful. She took another spoonful while she waited for him to continue.

"I lied to you, Claire."

Chapter 25

Dillon regretted the hurt he saw in her eyes, felt her guard go up like an invisible wall between them as her spoon stopped, poised over her bowl. He released the lock on the door to his past and pulled it open. "The first day we met, I told you I'd never been to Portland. That was a lie. When I was a cop, it was for the Portland Police Bureau."

"Why did you lie about it?"

"I made up my mind to forget that part of my life…forget the things I did."

She set her spoon down. "I'm listening."

Dillon spread his hands on the counter and stared at a spot between them, determined to get through it. He narrated the events by rote, the memory already too close to the surface. "I'd been on the force almost ten years, joined shortly after getting out of high school. I intended to make a career out of it. Then late one afternoon, my partner, Dean, and I responded to reports of a domestic dispute at an apartment complex. It was raining like hell." Dillon looked toward the windows of his loft, expecting to see the rain, but the sun was shining. He frowned and returned his gaze to the spot between his hands. "We heard the screaming when we drove up." Shrill, plaintive, gut-wrenching screams. "We exited the patrol car and approached on foot. We were almost to the door when it opened and a woman stepped out. Her face was swollen, her blouse ripped. She saw us and shouted at us to hurry." *He's killing him!* "Dean asked her if she needed an ambulance, but she just kept screaming at us to hurry. I asked her if there were any weapons in the house. She indicated no. We announced ourselves and entered.

"A big man, about two hundred and fifty pounds, had his hands around the neck of a smaller man, pinning him to the wall, choking him." Disjointed images flashed through Dillon's memory. Dean flying across the room. The big man attempting to shove his way out the door and Dillon knocking him down. The small man gasping for air, then reaching behind his back. "The smaller guy pulled a handgun from his waistband and fired. Dean returned fire." A movement in his peripheral vision. Turning. "A third suspect on my left reached inside his pocket." He didn't remember pulling his service weapon, just that it had been in his hand. "I fired. My bullet hit him in the chest." Too young to call a man. When he looked up at Dillon there was confusion in his eyes. Then nothing. "He died almost instantly."

"Was he armed?"

Claire's words startled Dillon from his memories, and he looked up at her. "Yes. When he fell, a nine-millimeter semi-auto dropped from his hand."

He'd stared at the handgun by his foot. *Did I see it before I fired?* Then Dean handcuffed the big man. The smaller man was stretched out facedown, blood trickling from a hole in his pant leg, hands cuffed behind his back. Dillon had no memory of the smaller man being shot, just the sound of Dean's pistol going off next to his ear. *Which one of us hand-cuffed him?* He remembered staring at the dead body at his feet. Martin Sawyer. No priors. High school graduate.

"I killed a nineteen-year-old kid," he said, forcing the words past dry lips.

If his admission shocked Claire, she didn't let it show. Like the experienced criminal defense attorney she was, she maintained an impassive expression—no sympathy or disgust flickered across her face. Dillon remembered the client she'd told him about, the one who had beaten a family to death. It occurred to him that of all the people who might understand what he'd gone through, it would be someone close to the ugly side of the law.

"Were there any charges against you or your partner?" she asked.

"No. There was an investigation, but they didn't find any evidence of wrongdoing. Dean took time off to recover. I went back on the job as soon as they let me. I didn't want to sit at home thinking about it, figured it was better to put it behind me and get on with my routine." He drew in a heavy breath. "Then the nightmares began."

"Did you talk to anyone?"

"If you mean a shrink, no. I wanted to keep my job." Seeing

the department psychologist would have sent a signal of instability or weakness and opened the door for a fitness evaluation and possible termination. He'd seen it happen before. "My wife, Deb, tried to understand. So did my folks. But they thought I should be able to shake it off and get on with life, like everything was normal."

"But it wasn't."

"I started going out for a few beers after my shift." Letting off steam. Sharing war stories. His fellow officers had meant well when they said, *Hey, don't sweat it. The bastard was armed.* But the support wore thin, and it didn't change the fact that he'd killed a kid. "Eventually I moved to the hard stuff." He'd had a taste for bourbon. "If I stayed numb enough, *drunk* enough, I could face the next day, and the day after that. It wasn't long before my marriage fell apart. My parents disowned me. I lost my job. I figured I had two choices—put my service pistol to my head and end it, or start over as far away as possible, where nobody knew me or asked questions."

"Then I showed up, a criminal defense attorney, asking questions. Two strikes."

"Yes. Strike three was shooting at the moose. I've been carrying that damn revolver around, pretending I'm okay with it, but the trail into McGrath was the first time I actually fired it. I forgot how it felt, the recoil, the smell, the concussion on my ears." The look in Martin Sawyer's eyes as he died.

"And now the nightmares are back."

"Different versions of the same thing. I shoot but the suspect doesn't stay dead, chases me, grabs at me. I can't get away. I'm slipping on blood and empty pizza boxes."

"Pizza boxes?"

"The apartment was full of them. I haven't been able to

look at a pizza since without it turning my stomach. Damn shame, too. I used to love pizza."

"Pepperoni?"

He smiled a little around the edges. "Not much of a challenge there, counselor."

"Don't call me counselor," she said, though her tone lacked bite. "What happened to the woman?"

"She took off."

Claire nodded. "I'm just glad you're okay."

"Sometimes I wish I wasn't okay."

She fixed him with a narrowed look, as if prepared to argue. Dillon counted five weighted beats, dull thuds against the back of his eardrums, before he saw her shoulders sag.

"I felt that way," she admitted. "After my last case. I didn't like myself very much. It shook my confidence."

"That's the reason you took a leave of absence."

"Yes."

"Not your ex, the Hammertown guy?"

She snorted. "Not even close."

Her answer should have made him feel better, but it didn't. Nothing about the situation felt good. She had a promise to keep, a career to return to, and enough of an emotional burden to bear without adding his on top of it.

"You made the right decision," she said, "getting the hell out."

"Now it's caught up with me."

She slid to her feet and came to him, caressed his cheek, and planted a light, salty kiss on his mouth. "You're not alone," she told him.

He turned and pulled her between his thighs, his hands loose on her hips. "I want you, Claire, more than I've wanted or needed anybody in a long time. But Alaska's my home now. What happens when you go home?"

"We've got two days to figure something out. Let's not waste them."

The memory of her kisses had kept him warm during those cold nights on the trail. This time her mouth promised seduction and intimacy. Things he didn't have a right to, sensations he'd refused himself. He felt exposed even as he craved. "Are you sure?" he asked.

"Yes."

She would need time to process the things Dillon had told her, to grasp the full impact of his trauma. That their reasons for coming to Alaska were so closely entwined did not surprise her. She'd sensed a connection the first time they met. Her heart ached for him, longed to make things right. But now, other needs drove her and demanded her attention—the way he touched her, the way he looked at her.

Clothes discarded with fevered urgency left a trail from the kitchen island to the bed. The jukebox in the bar below pulsed a deep, sorrow-filled tune. His calloused hands covered her, explored her body the way she did his, the tenderness and passion in his touch unbearably sweet.

"Look at me," he whispered.

She did. His eyes—close, intense, unguarded—sent a flutter of panic through her. She didn't want to fall in love with him, but in that instant, she knew she already had.

"I want you to see what you do to me."

Heat rushed to her cheeks.

"I want you to remember," he said.

Always. I will always remember.

Afterwards, he held her to him until his body stopped trembling, then cradled her as he lay back on the mattress. She listened to the hammer of his heart against her ear, felt his chest rise and fall as his breathing slowed, and smiled. She hadn't felt this relaxed and satisfied in an eternity.

Soft pink light filtered into the room. She lifted her gaze to the windows and watched the color deepen and spread as the sun dipped below the horizon.

In the early hours before the Bering West opened for business, Dillon led Claire downstairs to raid the kitchen. "Are you sure Vic won't object?" she asked as she pulled a huge tub of potato salad from the fridge and nearly dropped it. "Jeez, what's in here? Concrete?"

"Vic's not big on giving out recipes. As long as the customers are happy, I don't ask."

Claire popped the lid off the container and spooned some potato salad onto the two plates he laid out. "Smells delicious. Got any more chips?"

"How about a couple reindeer dogs instead? It's like venison, but less gamey."

"Perfect."

"Onions?"

"Of course."

She took a seat at the table and watched him work. He wore a long white apron over his jeans and flannel shirt—tails loose, sleeves rolled—and moved with economic grace, engaged in a routine intimately familiar to him. Her skin warmed remembering another intimate side he'd been more reluctant to show. Two days wouldn't be nearly long enough with this man.

The snap and sizzle of onions hitting a hot grill yanked at her senses. Their aroma stirred a boisterous rumble in her stomach. To avoid drooling, she took a bite of potato salad. Pickles, celery, garlic, and…fresh basil? Did Vic have an herb garden? Small decorative clay pots lining a window at home, perhaps? The thought of the gruff-looking cook babying pots of herbs brought a smile to her face.

"Vic told you, didn't he?"

She dragged her eyes from the plate of food in Dillon's hand. "He said when the grill burst into flames, you let out a high-pitched shriek."

He grunted a laugh. "I did." Sitting next to her, he handed her a reindeer dog smothered in caramelized onions and nestled in a hoagie roll. "I saw my investment going up in smoke."

"It didn't help that you tried to swat out the flames with a dishtowel."

"Almost set myself on fire. I suppose he told you how he barreled in and saved the day."

"Of course." She took a huge bite of her hot dog. "Oh my God. This is fabulous."

"I've learned a few things about using a grill since then."

She could have reminded him of yesterday's burnt sausages, but she chose instead to take another bite and make appreciative sounds of pleasure. She finished half her meal before saying, "Tell me about Helen."

He paused midbite. "Did she make a move on your dad?"

"Big time. He looked like he was enjoying it, too."

"She's a hard worker. Got a heart the size of Alaska. Tends to get what she sets her mind to." He took a bite, chewed. "Would it be so bad if she got her way this time?"

"No. God no. It's just…unexpected. After all these years, to see Dad fall for somebody so unlike Mom…"

"He told me about her. Caroline."

Claire's breath hitched, yet the prick of sadness at hearing her mother's name was reassuring. She never wanted to forget. "Why would he do that?"

Dillon put his food down and met her gaze. "He wanted me to understand what keeping a promise means to you."

"Oh." *Dad only knows the half of it,* she thought.

"I'm sorry, Claire."

"Me too." She didn't have to ask what he meant. He had killed a man. In the instant it took a hammer to strike a firing pin, his world changed forever. She had defended clients who killed for less, men like Colin Spears—there, she'd said his name, at least to herself—who felt no remorse. But the trauma of taking another human's life would haunt Dillon to his grave. She'd seen it before, working in criminal defense. Killing someone altered a person's sense of self. She was thankful he'd found a way to exist with his moral pain, carved a niche for himself in this remote place. Survived.

He couldn't leave and she couldn't stay.

"What do we do about it?" he asked.

"You owe me a dance."

A light over the mirror cast rum, burgundy, and vodka prisms across the polished bar, making Claire think of downtown Portland after dark—how the city's lights reflected on the Willamette River separating west from east. She smiled as her gaze caught the multicolored glow of a Wurlitzer jukebox sitting at the edge of a dance floor barely large enough to accommodate three couples. "It's perfect."

"I'm glad you like it."

"Just so you know, I don't do the Texas Two-Step."

"Neither do I." He crossed to the jukebox, dropped in a coin, and punched a selection. Turning, he held his hand out to her as the opening chords of an Eric Clapton tune began.

Claire gave a light laugh. At Dillon's raised brow, she said, "I was listening to this song when I saw the nonexistent power line."

"I can change it."

"Please don't."

She went to him, laid her head against the beat of his heart, and moved with him, their bodies in fluid unison. She lost herself in the lyrics of the song. As Clapton crooned about going home with his beloved, she thought, *I'm already there.* This was her home, here in Dillon's arms. She tipped her head and kissed his neck, felt his pulse trip a beat. He missed a step. She marveled at how that was all it took—a light press of her lips, a whispered word, a look—to ignite passion, to play havoc with a person's balance. His hand cradled her back and she felt the desire in his touch. She nipped his chin, his jaw.

"I thought you wanted to dance."

"I changed my mind."

He dipped his head and claimed her mouth. The force

rocked her, and she clung to him as his kiss skewed her own equilibrium and weakened her knees.

"Let's go upstairs," he murmured.

"I don't think I can make it."

"All right."

He drew her with him to the floor.

Chapter 26

Claire couldn't believe the number of people packed into Nome's recreation center for the Iditarod awards banquet the following afternoon. Mushers—joined by their families and friends—as well as volunteers and race fans sat around dozens of linen-covered tables. Iditarod Trail Committee officials announced awards and distributed trophies from a podium onstage. The room burst into applause as the first-place winner came up and spent fifteen minutes thanking everyone, including his team. Cameras flashed nonstop. Finishers in the top twenty split a $500,000 purse. Claire and Dillon each received a commemorative belt buckle and a check for $1,049, symbolizing the length of the Iditarod Trail.

There seemed to be no end to the awards: Most Improved Musher, Golden Harness, Humanitarian and Sportsmanship awards, Mushers' Choice, Rookie of the Year, Checkpoint of the Year, and Fastest Time from Safety to Nome. The Red Lantern could not yet be awarded: it would be presented to the final musher to cross under the burled arch, and two mushers were still making their way to Nome.

They shared tales from the trail and dined on prime rib, king crab, and gallons of strawberries. Locals—some of them regulars at the Bering West—stopped to congratulate Dillon. Claire was filled with a sense of community, of being part of an exclusive club.

She looked over at Dillon. *I love him.* Happiness threatened to overwhelm her as she thought of waking this morning in his bed, his body radiating warmth, his arm over her. Letting him cook breakfast for her. Showering together. She'd gone with him to take care of his dogs. Frank Johnson's kennel yard was small, with only a couple dozen assorted huskies and mutts. Bonnie and the rest of Dillon's team looked healthy and happy. Claire loved Frank instantly—a big man with wild red hair and a beard to match, a ready smile, and an even readier laugh.

"If the boss had warned me he was bringing company, I'd have put on my best overalls," he said with a chortle. "Least I can do is offer you a cup o' java."

"Putting a fancy name on it won't make that mud you brew any more drinkable," Dillon remarked. But his tone was good-natured, as though they'd shared this conversation countless times.

"I like my coffee to *mean* something," Frank said, striking a pose that reminded Claire of a Shakespearean actor and made her laugh.

She'd not only fallen in love with an Alaskan man—she'd fallen in love with the entire state and its people. They felt like family. A fist tightened around her heart. She'd told Dillon they had two days to figure something out, but there was no solution. By this time tomorrow, she'd be in Talkeetna packing for her return to Portland, and Dillon would stay in Nome. Where he belonged.

"Hey." Dillon's hand on hers drew her back, concern in his blue eyes. "Are you all right?"

"Don't worry," she said, forcing a smile, "I'm not going to faint this time."

"You're stronger than you look."

Tears threatened to push through her smile as her mama's words came back to her. *Can you be strong for me?* "Right now, it doesn't feel that way."

Chapter 27

Dillon stared out across Front Street at the seawall. Early morning light cast its soft promise over Claire sleeping in his bed a few feet away, her head cradled in the crook of one arm, her hair spilled across his pillow.

Things had changed between them last night. There wasn't the same explosion of heat and passion—instead, every moment had become precious. He felt it in the way she touched him, her fingers lingering as though committing him to memory. As though their time together was something fragile to preserve.

He took what she gave, held it in his heart, and gave in return, knowing the more they shared, the harder it would be to do the right thing. To let her go. His head was fucked up. If she stayed, he risked alienating her the way he'd alienated the people he'd left behind in Portland. His past was scarred with regret. It screamed at him. It was Deb's voice, screaming at him for coming home drunk again, for being gone at all hours and not telling her where he'd been. It was his dad's voice raised in anger: *You're not welcome in this house!* It was Martin Sawyer's mother screaming at him in the police station for murdering her son. How long would it be before he gave Claire a reason to scream? He didn't think he could survive that. The only way to prevent it was to suppress his feelings and let her go.

She stirred in her sleep. He resisted the urge to go to her, lie beside her, and hold her. Time was too short. He felt her absence creeping nearer.

Claire found herself alone in the bed when she woke. Daylight filtered into the apartment through the open shutters. She glanced at the alarm clock. Her plane left for Anchorage in two hours.

Dillon stood looking out the window with a mug in his hands. He wore last night's jeans and gray sweatshirt, the sleeves pushed to his elbows. Claire wrapped a blanket around herself and went to him. He didn't protest when she took the mug from him and sipped the dark coffee. It was cold. She lifted her eyes to meet his. "Did you get any sleep?"

"A little."

"Another nightmare?"

The look he gave her tore at her. "I've been pretending everything's normal, but it's not. I'm not. Or I'd get on that plane with you instead of hiding in Nome."

"Hiding?"

"What would you call it?"

"Surviving. You started over, got sober, then chose to test yourself every single day by owning a bar, for God's sake."

"None of which changes the fact that I killed a nineteen-year-old boy."

"That boy might've killed you if you hadn't shot first."

His jaw tightened. "We'll never know, will we?"

Tears welled in her eyes despite her vow to not, under any circumstances, cry. "What do you want to do, Dillon?"

"Push rewind. Freeze time. Hell, I don't know." His calloused hand cupped her face.

Claire felt his lips tremble as they met hers. In that moment she forgave him for letting her go, for being the strong one.

Dillon cherished the touch, the taste of her. Then he watched her pack and took her to the airport. Her plane was already boarding when they arrived.

"If there's anything I can do to help," she told him, the determined angle of her chin not quite steady, "you know where to find me."

"No," he said softly. He didn't want her waiting for him. He had failed himself. He had failed his family. He would fail her. "I'm sorry, Claire."

Her chin remained determined, even as a tear ran down one cheek, then the other. "No regrets," she said.

Unable to speak, afraid of the despair closing his throat, Dillon kissed her and watched her go.

Chapter 28

Claire stood in the middle of the garden she and her mother put in so many years ago, a light spring rain pattering on the hood of her waterproof jacket. After leaving Nome, she compartmentalized her emotions in order to disconnect from Alaska and re-enter the life she'd left behind. A life without the Sommer family, without the dogs, without Dillon. She'd told him no regrets, but she had one: that she hadn't tried harder to hold onto him. He'd made it clear he wanted a clean break, and that's what she was determined to give him. She had thrown herself into her work at the firm, floundered as she tried to fit in and feel like she belonged there. She filled her meager time off with errands in an attempt to reconnect with the rhythm of city life. But Portland lacked the comfort of home she had hoped for. Only here in the garden, where her childhood memories were the strongest, could she get close.

Mud sucked at her faded pink galoshes. They'd been waiting by the door of the covered patio where she left them two years ago. Planting season was still at least a month off, the vegetable cages and trellises stowed in the shed, the raised beds sprouting dandelions and clover. Over the years there had been countless varieties of tomatoes, pole beans, beets, hot and mild peppers, zucchini, half a dozen different greens, and cucumbers—especially lemon cucumbers—produced in this fifteen-foot square plot.

Claire remembered picking the first pumpkin grown by her own hands. Her mother baked and pureed the pulp for pies, and it was tradition to let one pumpkin grow as large as possible so it could be carved into a jack-o'-lantern for Halloween. The year Claire was able to handle the carving tools without help, Mama had begun to grow weak from the cancer treatments. The brightly patterned scarf tied around her thinning hair made her skin appear sallow, almost transparent. It had frightened Claire. She remembered tears dripping from her chin onto the pumpkin she was carving.

"Don't be afraid, honey."

Claire knew people who grieved over not recalling the sound of a deceased loved one's voice, but she heard the gentle inflection of her mother's words as if they had been spoken just yesterday. Mama had dried her face with a dishtowel and said, "I plan to be around for a very long time."

"Promise?"

There'd been the slightest hesitation in her mother's response. Claire hadn't noticed it as a young girl in misery, but looking back now, she saw it with the clarity of maturity and time.

"I promise," Mama said. "But I might need your help to take care of Daddy until I get better. Can you do that? Can you be strong for me?"

"Yes, Mama. I promise."

She hadn't felt strong, but she had promised, hoping it would make Mama better. She never told her dad; it was a secret held dear. Her dad thought she had returned because of her promise to him, but it was the one she made to her mother all those years ago that called her home.

After Mama's death, Alice, the stay-at-home mom next door, had offered to help work the garden plot in exchange for a share of the harvest. Even during Claire's time in Alaska, Alice turned soil, set up trellises, planted seeds. With her help, the garden continued to thrive year after year, a living legacy to the mother Claire still missed.

By the end of her second week back at home in Portland, Claire found a one-bedroom apartment within walking distance of the house—just far enough to give her breathing room.

"It's small," her dad commented when he helped her move a few of her belongings out of storage. The rest would stay in storage until she decided what to do with it. Too much of it reminded her of Grant and would be donated or sold.

"It's all I need."

Her time in Alaska taught her that. Her physical requirements had simplified: a place to sleep, a place to eat, a place to bathe. The rest would take longer.

Chapter 29

She shouldn't be here. He watched bloody fingers grab her from behind, begin choking her. He tried to pull her free, save her, but his hands passed through her ghost-white figure and he lost his balance, staggered. She struggled to breathe, her wild eyes pleading for help. He lunged and fell again, slipping in the blood on the floor. Not the floor, snow. Cold. Red. Red with her blood. *God, she needs to get out! She's going to die and I can't save her. No!*

Dillon jolted awake and realized he had fallen out of bed and was sitting on the floor. A sick knot in his stomach pushed its way up his throat. He forced himself to look over his shoulder at the tangled sheets, terrified he'd see Claire's bloodied, lifeless body.

She wasn't there.

The knot shifted to his heart. She never would be.

Two weeks and the nightmares were getting worse. Two weeks and the hole in his heart from Claire's leaving had become an overwhelming void. He saw her everywhere, not just in his nightmares: in shop windows, down grocery aisles, sitting at a table in the diner. He ached for her. He was falling apart and he didn't know how to stop it.

"Oh God," he groaned, raking his hands through his hair. "I miss you, Claire."

"Got a minute, boss?"

Dillon flinched and looked up to find Vic standing in the office doorway sans his customary stained white apron. *Quitting time already?* A glance at the desk clock confirmed the diner had locked up an hour ago. "Come in. I'm—" His gaze dropped to the timesheet in front of him. It was upside down. *Like my life.* "Finished." He slid the timesheet aside.

Vic entered the closet-sized office and closed the door.

Aware of his cook's claustrophobia, Dillon straightened. "That serious, huh?"

"You tell me." Vic pulled the room's lone folding chair around and straddled it, resting his thick arms across the back. "Kristi left in tears this afternoon."

"Ah, hell." The starch went out of Dillon's shoulders. He'd been nursing a killer headache from lack of sleep and was already in a foul mood when his young waitress waltzed into work that morning with lime-green hair. The stark color hit him like a knife to both eyeballs. He couldn't recall his exact words, but he remembered the hurt look she had given him. He'd acted like a first-class asshole. "I'll talk to her tomorrow."

"If she comes back. What's up with you, man? The girl's only nineteen. Cut her some slack for wanting to express herself."

Nineteen. The same age as Martin Sawyer. Dillon glanced at the closed office door, felt the walls press in on him. He took a long, deep breath and focused on a spot in the middle of his desk. "I said I'll talk to her."

"You haven't been sleeping, have you?"

The observation caught Dillon off guard. *Sleeping?* He worked longer hours at the diner. He spent more time with the dogs. None of it helped. He couldn't sleep without the night terrors, so he stopped trying. "It's like this after every race, you know that," he told Vic tightly.

"Yeah, yeah. I know how the race screws with your sleep and it takes a while to get back to normal." Vic grunted. "Whatever the hell *normal* is." His eyes narrowed. "But this time is different. It's been almost a month. Everybody can see your fuse getting shorter. Something happened out there on the trail that's eating your insides."

Dillon resented being cornered by his own fallibility. "If I wanted a shrink," he said, his words sharp, "I'd hire one."

"No, you wouldn't. That's not what we do."

"We?"

"Wounded warriors, disabled vets, fucked-up soldiers."

"You've got the wrong guy. I've never been in the military."

"But you've served."

Sworn to protect. Dedicated to serve.

Vic nodded. "I see I've touched a nerve. What was your war zone?"

Dillon looked away, unable to hold Vic's gaze. But looking away drew his attention to how small and closed in the room was. Sweat prickled his skin. He needed air. He knew he wouldn't get past Vic until he gave him an answer. "I was a Portland police officer." The words raked his throat.

"Explains why you let Claire go back to Portland alone."

"She had a—"

"Who'd you kill?"

Vic may as well have reached across the desk and back-handed him. "None of your God damn business."

Vic shrugged. "You can talk to me or you can find your-self another cook. I'm not sticking around to watch you self-destruct."

"Go to hell."

"Already been there, man."

Chapter 30

You'll never be the same when it's over.

A tremor of panic snaked through Claire as the truth of Dillon's words taunted her yet again. She looked around her office at the floor-to-ceiling bookshelves, the dark leather armchairs and matching couch on a sage-colored carpet, the rain-spattered window overlooking downtown Portland and the Willamette River. She was unable to shake the restlessness beating inside her as persistent as the falling rain. It had been an uncharacteristically wet June. She and Alice had replanted the lemon cucumbers a week ago because the first seeds had drowned.

A headache drilled into her temple. She glanced at the

Madison file on her desk. It was a clear case of self-defense, but something was missing, a detail lurking at the edge of her awareness.

Three months and she still struggled to concentrate, still couldn't sleep longer than four hours at a time, still woke listening for the dogs. She felt suffocated by the fussy clothes, the shoes that hurt her feet, the business lunches, the court-room appearances, the prison consults, the city noise, the crowds of people pressed together. As hard as she tried, she couldn't force her life in Portland back into its comfortable niche. Pieces of it crumbled from under her a little more every day, like an eroding embankment.

She'd packed and unpacked half a dozen times with no destination in mind. Janey told her their door was always open, but Claire had no desire to take advantage of her friend's hospitality again.

Pushing away from the desk, she smoothed the front of her gray pin-striped skirt and paced. Window. Desk. Bookshelves. Window. She rubbed her throbbing temples. *What am I missing?*

Dillon. I'm missing Dillon. His voice, his touch, the way his intense blue eyes saw her for who she was and didn't try to change her. *How is he doing?* Three months and not a word. She'd picked up the phone twice but disconnected before completing the call both times. She wanted to believe that if something was horribly wrong, Helen would let her know. Her dad and Helen were in constant communica-tion—letters, phone calls, emails. If Helen ever mentioned Dillon, her dad remained annoyingly tight-lipped about it. He wouldn't talk about his relationship at all, telling Claire repeatedly that a gentleman doesn't kiss and tell until she felt like kicking him. There was no denying the light in his eyes.

Helen wasn't so unlike Mama in that regard—she made him happy, and Claire was happy for him.

She was happy for everyone but herself. She felt a full-blown pity party inviting her to open its doors and stay until dawn. Tempting.

She dragged her thoughts back to the Madison case. *I've been away too long. Things have changed. I've—*

"Claire?"

She stopped and glanced toward the door. *Great. Now I'm hallucinating.*

She looked fragile in her white silk blouse, her slim skirt showing enough leg to make Dillon's chest tighten. She fixed her dark eyes on him like a deer in headlights and the air in the room stilled, making it hard to breathe.

He should say something. Explain himself. What if she didn't want to see him? A boulder lodged in his stomach. "Am I interrupting?"

"It's really you."

"Guilty."

She took a halting step toward him but stopped. "What are you doing here?"

Looking for you. That was the easy answer. But his reasons for coming to Portland were a hell of a lot more complicated than his need to see her. "I'm through hiding."

"Good." She tucked her hair behind her ear, a gesture he found achingly endearing. "That's good."

He accepted her hesitation, knew he deserved it. Pulling in

an uncertain breath, he asked, "Is there a boyfriend I should know about?"

She gave a weak laugh. "God, no."

"Then would it be all right if I kissed you?"

The small cry she made was all the answer he needed. The heaviness in his stomach lifted, and he met her in two strides. He pulled her close, pressing his lips to hers as a hint of lavender seduced him—a new fragrance. It suited her. Her outfit, professional and feminine, suited her too. His calloused hands snagged at the back of her blouse, her slim curves familiar beneath the whisper of fabric.

"I've missed you," he said, and kissed her again.

He felt her breath hitch. Her fingers dug into the fabric of his shirt. "I've missed you too, damn it. Why didn't you at least call?"

"I'm sorry I shut you out."

"I don't need you to protect me."

"I know." He brushed her hair back from her face. "It's one of the things I love about you."

Tears made her eyes shine. "Then what's the problem? Talk to me, Dillon."

"I'm the problem, my screwed-up head. But I've been working on that."

She desperately wanted to believe him. He remained handsome in the rawboned way she remembered, but he looked rough around the edges, as though he'd had his share of sleepless nights. She worried that his nightmares had worsened.

His presence pulled at her—his smell, his touch—but she needed to know what she was up against before she exposed her heart to him again.

She pulled out of his arms, went to her desk, and called Maggie in the front office. "I'm going to be unavailable for the rest of the afternoon."

"Shall I cancel your dinner appointment?" Maggie asked.

"No. Dinner's still on."

Maggie exhaled in relief. "Excellent."

Claire hung up and gestured to the couch. "Have a seat."

"You've got a dinner date?"

"No. That's a code Maggie came up with. If I'd told her to cancel dinner, she'd have security in here so fast you wouldn't know what hit you."

He shot her a sharp look. "Has that happened?"

"Once." Claire resisted the impulse to smile at his chivalry. Maybe someday she'd tell him about the client who had scared the crap out of her and Maggie, but now wasn't the time. She joined him on the couch, sat on the edge so she could face him, close but not quite touching. She didn't need to touch him to feel the tension in his body. "Tell me what's going on."

He hesitated as though uncertain where to begin, his gaze focused on the space of cushion between them. "Things fell apart. I fell apart. Nightmares. Insomnia."

She didn't know how to ask if he'd started drinking again without sounding accusatory, so she held her tongue, took shallow breaths, and waited.

The look in his eyes sliced through her heart. "I wanted a drink so damn bad it scared me."

"What stopped you?" she asked, her throat thick with relief.

"Vic. He knew something was wrong. Hell, everybody did.

He dragged me to a place in Nome that helps people with post-traumatic stress disorder."

Claire nodded.

"You're familiar with it?"

"PTSD has been offered as a basis for defense. I haven't handled a case personally, but I did a little reading when I got home." Following a hunch, she had pored over books from the library and spent late hours researching the disorder online. She discovered PTSD was far more prevalent in law enforcement than she had ever realized, that police officers were expected to be compassionate yet invincible, and to never make mistakes. Just as Dillon had done, they tried to suck it up and keep going. She had watched videos that made her cry. But she understood Dillon needed a patient listener more than he needed tears and comfort right now. "How did Vic know?"

"He's a Vietnam veteran, been through it himself."

"I would never have guessed. He's such a big softy."

Dillon grunted. "Vic a softy? Are we talking about the same guy?"

"Anybody who tattoos the name of a beloved dog on his bicep is a softy in my book."

The look of surprise on Dillon's face made her laugh. "Reta is a *dog*?"

"An Aussie-husky mix and his constant companion for fifteen years." When Vic had spotted Claire, lost and weepy eyed after saying goodbye to her dad and the Sommers, he lifted her spirits with the story of Dillon's grill fire, then had her near tears again as he talked about his Reta girl. "He never told you?"

"I never asked."

Claire shook her head, scooted back onto the couch,

shoulder to shoulder with him, and took his hand. "He cares about you, Dillon. A lot of us do."

"I'm finally figuring that out." He lifted her hand and brushed his lips across her fingers. "I've been an idiot."

"Yeah, you have." She kissed the edge of the slanted smile he gave her. "So where do we go from here?"

Chapter 31

Dillon asked Claire to drive his rental. He'd been away from Portland too long; downtown traffic made him jittery and screwed with his concentration. Sitting in the passenger seat gave him a chance to see how the city had changed in his absence. New shops and eateries peppered Broadway around the Arlene Schnitzer Concert Hall—known to locals as The Schnitz. Rain filled gutters, pooled in potholes, dripped from awnings, and streaked the sides of bus shelters. People hunched under battle-weary umbrellas or ignored the weather altogether, going about their business with a posture of indifference. Those with no homes to shelter in continued to gravitate to Burnside—a reminder of how the city always seemed to come up short for those most in need.

All in all, not much had changed. Except him.

The car's wipers cleared the windshield every three seconds. Flashes of moments surfaced then disappeared as the city's images blurred and cleared and blurred again. His therapist had recommended cognitive behavioral processing, visiting reminders of his trauma, putting his feelings into context through exposure.

"The shooting, the damaged relationships, the alcoholism, all happened in Portland, correct?" she had asked him one dreary afternoon.

"Yes."

"How likely do you think you are to face similar situations if you return to Portland?"

Her question set him back. "I wouldn't do any of it again."

"Then stop running. Go to Portland, face the source of your fears, and your thinking patterns will change."

She called it desensitization, but now, riding in the car with Claire, the reminders were coming at him too fast. Hypervigilant, his brain wasn't able to process them. He felt his pulse quicken.

Claire stopped at a red light. "How are you doing?"

He met her gaze. He'd missed those eyes. The unguarded care in them calmed him. "I'm good."

But his calm didn't last. As they crossed the river and neared the address Dillon had given her, images slowed and sharpened. Details his memory had dulled came into clarity. The crumbling mini-mall with its laundromat, all-night convenience store, and take-out pizza. The chain-link fence along an embankment to the Banfield freeway. The low brick wall in front separating the parking area from the residential street. Claire pulled into a slot reserved for guests and shut off the engine. The drum of rain on the car roof rivaled the heightened pounding of his heart.

"Is this where it happened?"

"No." He drew in a long breath and blew it out. "Yes."

The building didn't look right. They say when you go back to a place after being away for years, things seem smaller. Maybe that was the case. Or maybe it was the new windows and the cream-yellow paint with white trim. The building of his nightmares no longer existed.

He opened the car door to the rush of noise from the freeway and waited for a brief flare of anxiety to subside before getting out. Claire followed, pulling the hood of her rain jacket over her hair. She linked her arm in his and walked the length of the building with him to the last apartment on the end: number six.

Details sped up again, bombarding him in quick flashes: a woman's scream, her torn blouse. Two men struggling. Dean firing. Intense ringing in his ears. A third man reaching into his pocket.

Naked fear.

The force of the realization hit him like a punch to the stomach. He fought to keep from vomiting, locking his knees to remain upright.

Claire's hold on his arm tightened. "Talk to me, Dillon."

Remember all the pieces to process the trauma and heal.

Warm rain soaked his cotton shirt, plastered his hair, and ran into his eyes, a baptismal rite as the marrow-deep terror he'd blocked out consumed him. "I thought I was going to die," he said, his voice raw.

He regretted taking the life of Martin Sawyer, would carry the burden of it to his last breath—but the instant before he pulled the trigger, the moment when he came face-to-face with his own mortality, tortured him more.

He'd masked his fear behind a lie so he could live with himself. The support from his coworkers turned the lie into an insatiable animal eating at his conscience. He drank to kill the beast. But the beast hadn't died; it had stowed away and followed him to Alaska, hibernating, waiting to expose his self-deception.

"I panicked and was treated like a hero for it." Saying it aloud made it something concrete he could face rather than cower from.

Claire didn't offer empty platitudes or attempt to console him. He appreciated her silent witness.

"I had no right to drag you into this," he said. "But I'm glad you're here."

"Me too." She looked up at him, rain dripping from her lashes. "Did it help, coming here?"

"Yes." It surprised him how easily the admission slid from his mouth.

A baby cried and a woman shouted, "Are you people lost or something?"

Dillon's attention swung to the source. Apartment six's door stood open, and he flinched.

But the woman watching them with a baby on her hip, her stance defensive, wore a baggy Oregon Ducks T-shirt, not a torn blouse. She was younger. The room behind her looked lived in and comfortable. There was carpeting where there had been stained linoleum, toys where there had been trash. Framed photos hung on the wall where the small man had once been pinned and choked.

More nightmare images evaporated, replaced by a lightness Dillon felt in his shoulders and in his psyche.

It was Claire who answered the young mother. "No, ma'am, just taking a walk down memory lane."

"Did you use to live here?"

Her frown told Dillon she was aware of the apartment's history. Or maybe she was simply protecting her home. Either way, she wanted them to leave. "No, nothing like that," he said. "Sorry to have bothered you."

"Well, okay then." She moved back a step and began to close the door. "Have a good afternoon."

"Thank you." He looked at the number on the door, really looked at it this time, and realized the peeling stick-on from his nightmares had been replaced with a shiny brass plate. How had he missed that earlier?

The curtain at the window stirred, and Dillon saw the woman peeking out at them. "We'd better leave," he said, "before she calls the cops."

Claire laughed, reached up, and kissed him. "Let's go to my place and get out of these wet things."

The hot water felt good on Claire's chilled skin. Dillon's touch felt better. Love washed over her as his hands lathered and caressed. No one had ever affected her the way this man did. She longed to reach him in the same way. Her earlier hesitation was gone as his weathered hands explored her with sweetness and open desire.

She took him to her bed, drew him into her body and heart, moved with him, raced with him, watched his eyes lose focus as he said her name.

"Thank you," he whispered, "for all of it."

She heard the relief in his voice, felt it in the way he held her. Claire cuddled against him, every bone, muscle, and hair follicle relaxed, even as her heart still drummed in her chest. "You're welcome."

They lay wrapped together for several long, sated minutes. Then she felt his body succumb to sleep, listened to the slow rhythm of his breathing. She held him and waited for the nightmare.

She was still waiting as she drifted off.

Chapter 32

Claire opened her eyes to the half-light of early evening and the smell of coffee. Dillon wasn't in bed. She pulled on her pink terry robe and found him in the kitchen wearing a dry change of clothes and setting out plates and soup bowls. An impressive amount of Chinese take-out boxes engulfed her miniscule dining table, and the coffee maker gurgled on the counter.

He glanced up and smiled. "Hope you're hungry."

"Famished." She took a seat. "You ordered delivery?"

"I wanted to order pizza," he admitted, "but I'm not there yet."

"Give it time," she told him softly. "Just being here is a

huge step." He had picked up their wet clothes and washed the dishes. "Did you get any sleep?"

"Like a baby, until hunger woke me." He poured two cups of coffee and brought them to the table. Then he opened the boxes of food and sat across from her. "Dig in."

The aroma of deep-fried pork and shrimp, chow mein, fluffy rice, and savory wonton soup made her stomach rumble. "Oh," she said around the first bite of shrimp. "Oh, this is good."

"Better than barbecue potato chips."

She grunted. "Not even close." She reached for another shrimp.

"Hey, slow down there."

"Just making sure I get my share before you wolf them all."

He gave her a slanted smile and grabbed another shrimp for himself.

They ate in blissful silence until Claire thought she would burst. She made space in the refrigerator for the leftovers and brought the coffeepot to the table. "Refill?"

"Please."

A feeling of rightness settled over Claire as she poured him coffee, her knotted, restless unease gone. It struck her that the missing element she'd struggled with earlier in the day had been herself. The Madison case was solid, but she had checked out.

"Did you know Dad and Helen have been writing?" she asked, returning the pot to the counter.

"It's all she talks about. She's going to be mad as hell when she finds out I came here without saying anything."

Claire smiled as she pictured Dillon being confronted by Helen's daunting bosom thrust out in anger. "Believe it or not, Dad's talking about another visit to Alaska."

"Tell him the sea ice is melting."

She let out a hoot of laughter. "He'll be relieved to hear it."

"This is nice," Dillon said as she rejoined him at the table. "You and me."

"Yes. It is." She sipped her coffee, the question of their own uncertain future together at the forefront of her mind. "When's your flight back?"

"I don't have one."

Her coffee mug paused midair. "What do you mean?"

"I didn't buy a return ticket." He reached out and set her mug on the table, then took her hand. "I love you, Claire. If living in Portland is what it takes to have you in my life, I'm willing to stay."

It was sweet of him to offer. Totally unnecessary, but sweet.

"This isn't where my sled is parked," she told him. She couldn't remember who said it—that a musher's home is where their sled is parked—but hers was in Alaska. She knew that much for certain now. It may have happened when she looked up and saw Dillon standing in her doorway this afternoon, but her heart told her she'd known it much earlier. The *when* of it didn't really matter. She'd fallen in love with an Alaskan man. He may have come from Portland, but the Last Frontier was in his blood as much as it was in hers.

He released her hand and sat back. "What about your dad?"

In place of the anxiety his question would have stirred three months ago, a comfortable peace filled her. "Daddy's in love," she said, and smiled. "He'll understand."

"And the law firm? Your career? Becoming a *law partner?*" Dillon gave a teasing grin.

Claire tossed a wadded napkin at him. "I never said I

wanted to become a partner," she pointed out, though at one time she had considered it. "The firm will survive without me. As for my career..." She shrugged. "I can practice law pretty much anywhere, if that's what I decide I want to do." Though right now, practicing law wasn't high on her list of priorities. Alaska called to her. The dogs called to her. And there was Dillon.

"You've been thinking about this awhile."

"Just the part about hating it here. The rest I'll take one checkpoint at a time."

He smiled a little, but she saw the hesitation in his eyes. "I won't lie to you. I'm not over it yet...the past."

A warning to give her the chance to change her mind. She knew he was closer to making peace with it—the trauma— than he gave himself credit for. The bar, the dogs, the support group, coming to Portland and owning his fear—it was his healing process. She felt a stab of sadness at the thought that he would try to put the entire load on himself.

She told him about the promise she'd made to her mother. Because he had a right to know. Because she needed him to realize they had both been carrying more than their share of emotional baggage. "I told Mama I'd take care of Daddy," she said. "That's the real reason I was adamant about coming home. But Helen has helped me realize I don't have to do it alone. And neither do you, Dillon." She met his gaze. "Your past doesn't scare me."

The hesitation in his eyes melted. "It's easier when you're surrounded by the right people."

"Yes, it is."

"Will you come back to Nome with me, Claire? Move in with me? Share my life?"

Her pulse stumbled, then raced. "What? I mean...that's

quite a leap." She had already made up her mind to return to Alaska—even Nome, so she could be close to him—but she couldn't help remembering how the last live-in arrangement had ended for her.

"Am I wrong to think you love me?" Dillon asked.

"No. God no. I do love you."

"But living together scares you."

"Yes. No. I don't know." She laughed at herself, fussed with the front of her robe.

"I don't want to push you into anything you're not sure of."

She stopped fussing. "I'm sure I love you."

"That's a good start." He came around the table, drew her to her feet, and wrapped his arms around her waist. "I'll give you candlelight and champagne every night if those things will make you happy."

She draped her arms around his neck. "You don't drink, remember?"

"I didn't say I'd join you. Even when I was drinking, I couldn't stand the bubbly stuff."

The look in his eyes, the slant to his smile, sent a rush of heat from the top of her head to her toes. Any reservations she may have had melted away, and a light laugh escaped her. "I don't need candlelight and champagne." She brushed her lips across his, whispered, "This is all I need," and kissed him. Intimate. Lingering. She felt his heart rate pick up. "But I have to admit, I wasn't expecting it."

"I'm full of surprises."

"I like surprises."

"You haven't answered my question."

Her pulse didn't stumble this time. She couldn't think of anything more right than sharing her life with this man. "The answer's yes, Dillon. I'll move in with you."

Air whooshed from him. "Hell of a surprise, counselor."

"I know where there's a cozy loft with a great view of the sunset."

"Sounds perfect," he murmured, and gave her a kiss that could warm the coldest Iditarod night.

Epilogue

The clouds had lifted overnight, bringing clear skies and sunshine. Dillon parked the rental car at the curb in front of his childhood home on Tillamook Street. Unlike the apartment complex from the day before, the two-story house with tan vinyl siding and faux-wood louvered shutters was just as he remembered. The blue spruce bordering the driveway looked fat and healthy—a Christmas tree he had helped his dad plant thirty years ago. Mom's roses bloomed scarlet, apricot, and lemon under the picture window.

The concrete pedestal birdbath planted midway across the lawn was new. A gray squirrel drinking from the birdbath's edge saw him approach and bounded off around the corner of the house, probably toward one of the many feeders Dillon knew his mom kept filled. He could still hear his dad grumbling about the small fortune they spent on critter feed, all the while tossing peanuts to any squirrel brave enough to get within range of his lawn chair.

Dillon had a lot of memories, good and bad, stored in this place. He remembered the tire swing in the back, his dad's small vegetable garden, his mom hanging up laundry while he helped. His mutt Spike loved to play in the sprinkler and followed him everywhere he went. They used to have a retired musician living on the block who played his sax in the evening, serenading the neighborhood. Spike always joined in, howling off tune.

Other sounds filled his head. Shattering glass. Mom's cry. Dad shouting at him to get out of the house and not come back until he was sober. The slam of the door.

Now that he was here, he wished he'd accepted Claire's offer to come along. He still couldn't believe she had agreed to move in with him. He'd do everything in his power to keep his mental shit from spilling over onto her, but it didn't scare him like it used to. This trip had been good for him. Claire was good for him.

His therapist had advised him to face his fear, keeping in mind the possibility of a payoff. "Claire will be there," he told her, though, at the time, he had no idea if she would even see him, much less want to help. He took a leap of faith, and Claire caught him. *Being here is a huge step.* Yes, it was.

And now he was taking another leap of faith, facing another fear. Would his parents allow him back into their lives, give him another chance? Would they even answer the door? The front drapes hung open, and his parents' Subaru sat in the driveway.

He started up the walk.

You're not welcome in this house.

His pulse hammered in his chest as he put one foot in front of the other. He reached the covered porch and grasped the wooden handrail. The third step gave a familiar groan. He caught the fragrance of peaches drifting from the roses and paused, pulling in a deep breath.

The doorbell had always been quirky, one of those things nobody ever seemed to get around to fixing. He would take care of it while he was in town, if they let him. His hand shook as he reached for the brass doorknocker. It thundered once, twice, three times.

Long seconds passed. Dillon sensed someone stealing a look at him through the peephole. The chain rattled free. The deadbolt snapped. The door pulled inward. The man regarding him with wary surprise from the other side of the screen looked smaller, his thick hair grayer. Dillon's heart squeezed at how much his dad had aged.

"Dillon?"

"Hi, Dad." *It's good to see you. I'm sorry I haven't called. How are you?* "I'm six years sober."

His dad nodded—a silent gesture of approval Dillon recognized. He felt another piece of his life shift back into place.

The screen swung open. "Welcome home, son."

Acknowledgments

I could not have written this book without the invaluable information provided by the official Iditarod website, champion Aliy Zirkle and her "Aliy Cam," numerous videos by other mushers, volunteers, and race fans, and a bounty of great articles and books published on the subject. There is so much more to the sport than what I have covered in these pages. Any discrepancies or errors are solely my own.

Deepest thanks to my mentor, Dorothy Burke Lopez, and a great group of writers at Mt. Hood Community College, whose critiques kept me honest and motivated through the early stages of development. Thank you to my beta readers: Kimberly A. Cook, Claudia DeGailler, Bettina Spencer, and my patient husband, Jack. My appreciation and love is boundless.

Working on this second edition with the talented, dedicated people at Ooligan Press has been a thrilling experience. I could not have asked for a more thought-provoking, intelligent team of editors, researchers, and designers. In particular, I want to thank publisher Abbey Gaterud, project managers Emily Frantz and Dani Nicholson, and copy chiefs Emma Hovley and Olivia Rollins. It's been an honor. My best to each and every one of you!

Anyone who is exposed to a terrifying incident that puts them in physical danger, or who is witness to a horrific event, is at risk of developing post-traumatic stress disorder: military and law enforcement personnel, firefighters, rescue workers, accident survivors, assault victims, people caught in natural or human-caused disasters, adults and children alike. I urge readers to learn more about PTSD, its symptoms, and its treatments.

About the Author

Writing in the spirit of adventure and happy endings, Cindy Hiday has won numerous honors, including first place in the Kay Snow Awards for Fiction from Willamette Writers. Her 2014 novel *Father, Son & Grace* (republished as *Destination Stardust* in 2019) is a Five-Star Readers' Favorite and a local book club choice. Cindy draws inspiration from the beautiful state of Oregon, where she lives with her husband and four-legged friends. When she isn't hard at work on her next novel or mentoring the latest group of writing talent as a part-time instructor for Mt. Hood Community College, Cindy enjoys hiking, gardening, and traveling. Follow her online at www.cindyhiday.com.

Ooligan Press

Ooligan Press is a student-run publishing house rooted in the rich literary culture of the Pacific Northwest. Founded in 2001 as part of Portland State University's Department of English, Ooligan is dedicated to the art and craft of publishing. Students pursuing master's degrees in book publishing staff the press in an apprenticeship program under the guidance of a core faculty of publishing professionals.

Project Managers

Dani Nicholson

Emily Frantz

Editing

Olivia Rollins

Emma Hovley

Design

Denise Morales Soto

Jenny Kimura

Digital

Megan Crayne

Kaitlin Barnes

Marketing

Sydnee Chesley

Sydney Kiest

Social Media

Faith Muñoz

Sadie Verville

Book Production

Andre Cole

Erica Wright

Courtney Young

Callie Brown

Nif Lindsay

Katherine Petersdorf

Bryn Kristi

Elle Klock

Kendra Ferguson

Des Hewson

Faith Martinmaas

Maegan O'Brion

Ruth Robertson

Siri Vegulla

Megan Huddleston

Bayley McComb

Laura Mills

Melinda Crouchley

Claire Meyer

Kimberley Scofield

Giacomo Ranieri

Gina Walter

Hannah Boettcher

Selena Harris

Grace Hansen

Scott Fortmann

Colophon

Iditarod Nights is set in Adobe Caslon Pro and Kumlien Pro. Designed by Carol Twombly, Adobe Caslon Pro is a revival of the pages printed by William Caslon between 1734 and 1770. Kumlien Pro was designed by Kevin King and Patrick Griffin for Canada Type and is a revival of the 1943 typeface by Swedish book designer Akke Kumlien.